SHIPMENT ONE

Tex Times Ten by Tina Leonard
Runaway Cowboy by Judy Christenberry
Crazy for Lovin' You by Teresa Southwick
The Rancher Next Door by Cathy Gillen Thacker
Intimate Secrets by B.J. Daniels
Operation: Texas by Roxanne Rustand

SHIPMENT TWO

Navarro or Not by Tina Leonard
Trust a Cowboy by Judy Christenberry
Taming a Dark Horse by Stella Bagwell
The Rancher's Family Thanksgiving by Cathy Gillen Thacker
The Valentine Two-Step by RaeAnne Thayne
The Cowboy and the Bride by Marin Thomas

SHIPMENT THREE

Catching Calhoun by Tina Leonard
The Christmas Cowboy by Judy Christenberry
The Come-Back Cowboy by Jodi O'Donnell
The Rancher's Christmas Baby by Cathy Gillen Thacker
Baby Love by Victoria Pade
The Best Catch in Texas by Stella Bagwell
This Kiss by Teresa Southwick

SHIPMENT FOUR

Archer's Angels by Tina Leonard
More to Texas than Cowboys by Roz Denny Fox
The Rancher's Promise by Jodi O'Donnell
The Gentleman Rancher by Cathy Gillen Thacker
Cowboy's Baby by Victoria Pade
Having the Cowboy's Baby by Stella Bagwell

SHIPMENT FIVE

Belonging to Bandera by Tina Leonard
Court Me, Cowboy by Barbara White Daille
His Best Friend's Bride by Jodi O'Donnell
The Cowboy's Return by Linda Warren
Baby Be Mine by Victoria Pade
The Cattle Baron by Margaret Way

SHIPMENT SIX

Crockett's Seduction by Tina Leonard
Coming Home to the Cattleman by Judy Christenberry
Almost Perfect by Judy Duarte
Cowboy Dad by Cathy McDavid
Real Cowboys by Roz Denny Fox
The Rancher Wore Suits by Rita Herron
Falling for the Texas Tycoon by Karen Rose Smith

SHIPMENT SEVEN

Last's Temptation by Tina Leonard
Daddy by Choice by Marin Thomas
The Cowboy, the Baby and the Bride-to-Be by Cara Colter
Luke's Proposal by Lois Faye Dyer
The Truth About Cowboys by Margot Early
The Other Side of Paradise by Laurie Paige

SHIPMENT EIGHT

Mason's Marriage by Tina Leonard
Bride at Briar's Ridge by Margaret Way
Texas Bluff by Linda Warren
Cupid and the Cowboy by Carol Finch
The Horseman's Son by Delores Fossen
Cattleman's Bride-to-Be by Lois Faye Dyer

The rugged, masculine and independent men
of America's West know the value of hard work,
honor and family. They may be ranchers, tycoons
or the guy next door, but they're all cowboys at heart.
Don't miss any of the books in this collection!

Cowboy
at
Heart

BABY LOVE

VICTORIA PADE

USA TODAY Bestselling Author

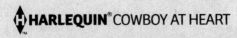

HARLEQUIN® COWBOY AT HEART

Recycling programs
for this product may
not exist in your area.

ISBN-13: 978-0-373-82617-9

BABY LOVE

Printed in U.S.A.

VICTORIA PADE

is a *USA TODAY* bestselling author of numerous romance novels. She has two beautiful and talented daughters—Cori and Erin—and is a native of Colorado, where she lives and writes. A devoted chocolate lover, she's in search of the perfect chocolate-chip-cookie recipe. For information about her latest and upcoming releases, and to find recipes for some of the decadent desserts her characters enjoy, log on to www.vikkipade.com.

To Andrew Immordino, for all his antics,
and to his Nana Mo and Papa Jo
for telling the stories.

Chapter One

"Got me some news," Buzz Martindale announced to Tallie Shanahan as Tallie made him do five more leg lifts than he wanted to.

She knew distraction was what the old wrangler had up his sleeve. As nurse, midwife and physical therapist in the small town of Elk Creek, Wyoming, she'd been visiting the McDermot ranch every day for the past three weeks to put elderly Buzz through his paces. Buzz had broken his knee shortly before Tallie had returned to her hometown and become the sole provider of medical care for the close-knit community that had recently lost its only doctor.

"Four more, Buzz," she persisted, ignoring his lure. But not without difficulty.

"Got me some news 'bout Ry," he added, upping the ante.

Okay, so it sparked some curiosity in Tallie. It wasn't as if she—and the rest of Elk Creek—hadn't been wondering what was going on with

Buzz's grandson Ry McDermot. Ry had received a mysterious and sobering phone call and hightailed it out of town without a word to Buzz or anyone else except to say he was leaving Buzz in the care of their housekeeper and Tallie. That had been a full week ago, and although Tallie had tried not to ask *every* day if Buzz had heard from Ry, she'd rarely managed to get through a session of Buzz's rehabilitation exercises without saying *something*.

"Three more," she instructed the wily old man, who was dressed in boxer shorts, a ratty bathrobe, even rattier cowboy boots and a hat that his housekeeper—Junebug Brimley—wanted desperately to burn.

"Ry's comin' home," Buzz said in almost a taunt. "On his way right now. Should be here any minute."

Tallie couldn't help the glance that shot itself toward the door as if Ry might, indeed, have just stepped up to it. In the process she lost the gentle grip on the elderly man's ankle that urged the lower half of his injured leg into its slow rise.

Buzz chuckled as if he could see right through her.

"Two more will do it for today, and then I'll rub that horse liniment into your knee," she said.

"Guess he's been in Cheyenne," Buzz offered.

"With Shane and Maya on their honeymoon?" she asked, the words spilling out on their own.

"Ry and Shane might be twins, but I don't think ole Shane needed Ry along on that," Buzz said with a sly laugh.

"Well, at least now you know where he's been," Tallie said as if she hadn't lost a minute wondering about it herself.

"Says he's bringin' home a sur-prize. A big 'un. But he didn't sound too happy about it."

"That so?" Tallie responded, still pretending she didn't have the slightest interest in anything to do with Ry.

But she *was* just pretending. The truth was that she had an inordinate interest in everything about Ry McDermot.

Not that she wanted it that way. She didn't. In fact she fought like mad against it. Fought like mad so the no-nonsense, keep-to-himself cowboy wouldn't guess that the highlight of her move back to Elk Creek had been the few times she'd talked to him about his grandfather's injury and recuperation.

She hadn't admitted that to a living soul. She didn't even want to admit it to herself. But old Buzz seemed to have sensed it.

Or maybe he just noticed how her eyes were always wandering to the door, watching for Ry, wondering if she might see him before each therapy session ended.

"Okay. That's five," she said then, removing the one-pound weight she had secured around Buzz's calf just above the boot top. "Where's the liniment?"

Medically speaking, Buzz's home-made concoction of horse liniment really wasn't doing anything. But she humored him every day by rubbing some of it into his knee. He insisted it made him feel better. Most likely the massage was what did the trick after the tiring exercises designed to rebuild his strength. But she didn't begrudge him that. She liked the old cuss.

Besides, it gave her an excuse to spend a few more minutes there. A few more minutes that increased her chances of running into Ry...

"There you go," she said when she'd finished with the liniment, too. She wasn't in a hurry to leave—although as busy as she was without a doctor in town, she should have been—but there was no more reason to delay. No reason but one. "I'll wash my hands and get going."

She snatched up her purse on the way to the bathroom connected to Buzz's room, hoping he didn't notice. Or realize why she wanted it with her. And rather than leaving the door open as she usually did, she closed it behind herself as if she wanted to use more than the sink.

She did.

She wanted to use the mirror, too. Just in case.

So after washing her hands, she took a comb from her purse and ran it quickly through her springy, pale blond hair. She kept the style short, only a few inches long on top and on the sides, letting it grow just past her collar in back because otherwise the natural curls became an unruly bush. Even so, her hair wasn't tame. Years ago she'd had to give up the notion of ever having sleek, sophisticated locks.

But then a sleek, sophisticated hairdo wouldn't have gone with her face.

Cute and perky—that was how her looks had always been described. It was better than being called homely and drab, but still the description didn't thrill her.

She'd always wished for a face that was classically beautiful. More refined. Stunning. But what she had was very white skin, eyebrows that matched her hair, a small, turned-up nose, lips she wished were fuller than they were and cheeks that didn't even hint at high bones or gaunt model's hollows.

Not that hers was a fat face. It wasn't. She'd been blessed with an enviable metabolism that kept her five feet four inches thin even when she overate or indulged herself. It's just that she was…cute and perky.

She did have good eyes, though, she reminded herself as she freshened her mascara. There was nothing about her eyes she would have changed. As far as she was concerned, they provided the only color she had—a blue the shade of the sky just before a spring storm, bright and dark at once. Thank heaven for small favors.

She dug a tube of lipstick out of the bottom of her purse then, telling herself she was being silly, that the odds of running into Ry in the next five minutes were nil. But still she applied the barely pink tinted gloss, again hoping that Buzz didn't realize she'd been in there sprucing herself up just in case she met Ry on her way out.

To justify the time she'd spent behind the closed door, she flushed the toilet, rewashed her hands and returned to the bedroom where Buzz was grinning like a Cheshire cat, as if he'd known all along what she was up to.

"He just parked out front," the old man informed her.

"Who?" Tallie asked, playing dumb while her pulse kicked into overdrive at just the assumption that Buzz was referring to his grandson.

But the elderly cowpoke never let her get away with anything. "You know who—Ry. He left his truck at the train station when he took off, and I just heard it outside. He's home!"

"That's nice. I'm sure you'll be glad to have him back. Especially with Junebug feeling under the weather. Now she can have that time off she needs."

"Ha! I'm not the only one who'll be glad to have 'im back," the old man said with a laugh.

Tallie began to gather up her exercise mat and weights, all the while listening much too intently for the sound of the front door opening. And telling herself to cool it, that she wasn't interested in Ry McDermot. Or any other man, for that matter.

But the moment she heard the front door actually open, she felt a rush of excitement that she couldn't hold down to save her life. And she ended up with her hands frozen on the handles of the athletic bag she used to carry her things, her gaze stuck like glue to the doorway and her heart beating in unison with each heavy footfall of cowboy boots across the entryway's tiled floor.

And then there he was.

Her eyes rose, taking in that first glimpse of hair that was barely brown and bleached by the sun with streaks that were nearly as light as hers. He wore it close to his head on the sides and back, longer on top where a natural wave carried it away from his face.

And oh, what a face it was!

Lean, angular, rawboned and ruggedly masculine, he wasn't fashion-magazine handsome, just staggeringly attractive in an all-man, rough-and-tumble, outdoorsy sort of way. He had a high forehead and a shelf of brow over eyes the bright green of kiwi fruit. Intelligent eyes that were deliciously incongruous with the hard-washed features of the cowboy, and shadowed by lashes so thick they hardly seemed real.

His nose was slightly long and thin, with a small ridge at the bridge and a pointed, slightly uneven tip. His upper lip was a mountain range of twin peaks with a deep valley in between, above a lower lip that was lush and turned Tallie's insides to mush every time she got a look at it.

His jawline was sharp, there was an indentation just off center in his chin and, as if his face weren't enough to dumbfound even the most savvy woman, he also had a strong neck, shoulders so broad they filled the doorway and commanded attention and a work-honed, muscle-laden body to die for.

But after losing herself in that first sight of him, Tallie's eyes refocused and took in more than the man himself. She suddenly realized that he had a backpack slung over one of those great shoulders, a bright-colored cloth bag held under one well-muscled arm, a suitcase dangling from that same hand and, carried like a saddle on his opposite hip, was what had to be his big surprise.

And a surprise it was.

For there, parallel to the floor, as if intent on the study of Ry's boots, was a little boy.

"What the—?" Buzz began but didn't seem able to finish.

Ry took a deep breath, breathed it out as if he were about to face a firing squad, set the three bags down and then swung the tiny tot to stand in front of him.

"This," Ry announced in a voice that echoed with what sounded like a mixture of his own shock, disbelief and dismay, "is Andrew."

Tallie guessed the tyke to be not more than eighteen or nineteen months old. He had a lot of straight wheat-colored hair cut neatly around a round-cheeked face. Big, bright blue eyes stared warily out as chubby fingers fiddled with each other. He was dressed in stubby tennis shoes, cuffed jeans, a striped T-shirt and a miniature jean jacket, and Tallie felt an instant craving to scoop him up into her arms.

But she didn't dare.

Andrew glanced up at Ry from over his wee

shoulder as if he didn't know what to make of the big man any more than Ry knew what to make of him. Then he looked from Tallie to Buzz, and out came his bottom lip at the same time the corners of his mouth went rapidly south.

Thinking fast and acting before the wail could reach the surface of that pout, Tallie reached into her carryall and pulled out a small, round, brightly colored Band-Aid. She dropped to her knees so she was closer to the baby's eye level, made quick work of unwrapping the Band-Aid and promptly thumbed it to the center of her forehead.

The corners of Andrew's mouth stayed pointing at his chin, but instead of crying he tentatively headed toward her on one of those crooked baby walks to see what she was doing with the second Band-Aid she'd taken from the bag.

He stopped before getting too close, and she held the bandage out to him.

"Hi, Andrew," she said in a soft, soothing, cheery voice.

He toddled nearer, looking suspicious but too intrigued to resist. When he got within reach, he pointed to his forehead and said something that sounded more like a grunt than a word.

Tallie got the idea. She pressed the Band-Aid

to his forehead while the tiny boy rolled those big blue eyes upward trying to see it. Then she pushed her athletic bag toward him, spreading the zippered top wide open so he could rummage inside as if it were a treasure chest, knowing there was nothing in it that could hurt him.

Once the distraction had succeeded, she looked back at Ry, who was watching with a forlorn expression on his face.

"What's goin' on, boy?" Buzz demanded.

"You know that phone call I got a week ago? Dirk Breckman and his wife were killed in a car wreck. This is their son. And they named me his guardian," Ry explained succinctly, his deep voice flat and matter-of-fact. But definitely not thrilled. "I spent the last seven days sorting through red tape and legalities—with the help of Maya, who probably didn't appreciate spending part of her honeymoon workin'—and here we are. A done deal."

A done deal that Ry was clearly uncomfortable with. He might be a big, strong, accomplished, successful, take-charge kind of guy, but it was obvious he was daunted by the prospect of sudden fatherhood. Daunted by the little boy himself. Not to mention that he was totally unprepared, ill-equipped and inept when it came to handling Andrew—Tallie had seen that for herself just in the way he'd carried him into the house.

"Glad you're here, though, Tallie," Ry said then.

It was a silly thing to note at that moment, but Tallie realized that it was the first time he'd ever said her name. And she wished she didn't like the sound of it so much.

But she did.

She tamped down on the feeling and raised questioning brows to him.

"Been thinkin' the whole way home. I'm gonna need some help with all this. I don't know my ass—head from a hole in the ground when it comes to these things. I'd like to hire you to help out."

There was no reason to feel disappointed. There was nothing that had gone on between them before, nothing he'd said or done since arriving home, to raise her hopes. Yet for some reason that simple comment about his being glad she was there must have struck a chord in her or why else would what had followed it have bummed her out?

Directly in front of her, Andrew had discovered the whole box of Band-Aids and was trying to figure out how to get the wrapper off a red strip.

Tallie smoothed a gentle hand across his hair

and stood ramrod straight to face Ry, putting an effort into smiling so he wouldn't know she'd had such a ridiculous reaction.

"I'm sorry, Ry, but my plate is full right now. It might be different if we had a doctor in town again, but as it is—"

"I'll pay you. Anything. Name your price."

"It isn't money. It's *time*."

"I'm desperate here," he admitted, sounding it. Looking it, too, as his eyebrows arched toward his hairline.

Something thrummed inside Tallie again.

Damn him, anyway, for the power to affect her with no effort at all! she thought.

"I suppose I could give you a few pointers. Help out where I can…*when* I can. And you could come to my parenting class," she said, thinking all the while that having more contact with him was probably not a good idea. Even if the prospect did send a little thrill through her.

"I don't know if that'll be enough."

"It's the best I can do."

"Take it," Buzz advised from his perch on the edge of his bed.

Apparently Ry considered it good counsel. "Can we start with some pointers right away? Because all I've got here for him is what's in these bags—some clothes and some doo-dads I don't know what to do with. I'm not set up for this…the whole house isn't set up for this. And I don't know squat about where to start."

He looked and sounded so rattled it was comical. Tallie's disappointment was dislodged and replaced by an inordinate need to laugh. How could a man like Ry, who could handle whole herds of cattle, a huge ranch, a business operation that produced the most sought-after beef in the world, and every catastrophe mother nature could throw at him, be daunted by this little bundle of boy?

Tallie fought not to let loose of the mirth that was building in her. "He didn't come with a crib or anything?"

"Nothin' but what I just carried in. I don't know what happened to whatever Dirk and Shelly had for him, but it didn't come with him. The foster mother did tell me not to bother with a crib, though. Said he climbs right out of 'em. But he fell asleep for about two minutes on the train seat and rolled right off onto the floor, so I don't know how he can sleep in a regular bed. Should I tie 'im into it or what?"

"No!" Tallie said in a hurry. "You can't tie him into bed. Look, I'll meet you at the baby shop in town and show you what you need. But I can't get there until just before it closes at seven tonight—I have appointments the rest of the afternoon. Think you can make do until then?"

As if to prove that she was asking too much, Andrew lost interest in the gym bag and the Band-Aids just then and started to cry—a loud, fussy, tired-sounding wail that made Ry's eyes close and his whole handsome face clench up.

But he didn't make a move to pick up Andrew, so Tallie did, swaying with him until he quieted while watching Ry with a wary eye.

"He's been doin' that cryin' thing at the drop of a hat for the last two hours. Over nothin'. I think he just doesn't like the looks of me."

The concern in his voice was edged with panic, and this time Tallie couldn't suppress a smile. She resisted the urge to assure him that nobody on earth could not like the looks of him and merely said, "Has he had any more than a two-minute nap?"

"No, not since they handed him over to me at eight this morning. Was he supposed to?"

"Babies need naps. Here's what you do. Push a bed into a corner, right up next to the walls, line some chairs up along the free side and the bottom so he can't fall out, change his diaper, give him something to eat, unless you've fed him already, and some milk. Try cold first, if he doesn't seem to like it, heat it just a little but test it to make sure it isn't hot enough to burn him—and then put him down—"

The horrified look on Ry's face stopped her.

Then it occurred to Tallie that the phrase *put down* to someone whose work was with animals meant something different than she'd intended.

Again she fought a laugh and amended, "Put him down for a *nap.* In the bed. He'll probably sleep straight through till it's time to meet me in town. When he gets up, change his diaper again—do you know how to do that?"

"The foster mother showed me."

"Good. Then change his diaper again and come into town. Do you have a car seat for him?"

"I strapped him in good and tight with the seat belt and a length of rope I had in the truck. He didn't like it, though."

"Well, do that again but drive carefully. It's dangerous for him not to have a safety seat."

Tallie could tell she'd already given as many instructions and cautions as Ry could absorb for the moment. Especially in the mild state of shock he seemed to be experiencing. Besides, she thought she'd told him enough to get him through the next few hours.

Still, she added, "Buzz raised your mother. He must have some—"

"Not me," the old man put in forcefully. "Babies was woman's work. All's I ever did was give 'er a bounce on my knee. Never changed a diaper or wiped a nose in my life."

"Well, if worse comes to worst, bounce Andrew on your good knee," Tallie said, giving in to a laugh at the sight of Buzz staring at Andrew as if the baby were a space alien.

Tallie checked her watch. "I'm late," she informed the room in general.

Going to Ry, she handed Andrew to him, seeing the clumsiness that said he was more at ease carrying the little boy like a saddle.

And as for Andrew, he didn't seem any more relaxed with Ry. Even perched on the big man's hip he reared back to put some distance between them and screwed up his face in preparation for another wail.

Tallie rubbed the baby's back to forestall it. "Hold him like you aren't afraid of him—it'll make you both feel better."

She took Ry's free hand, trying to ignore the warm feelings that flooded through her at that contact, and placed it on Andrew's back where her hand had been a moment before, urging Ry to bring the little boy in closer.

He did, mimicking her massage, albeit stiffly.

"Think of him as a skittish mare," she suggested.

That seemed to help as Ry appeared to

relax—if only slightly—and use a more sure hand in rubbing Andrew's back.

The tired Andrew laid his head on Ry's shoulder and stuck the knuckle of an index finger in his own mouth to suck.

Tallie watched as Ry's expression turned surprised and his oh-so-attractive and troubled face was infused with a kind of shy pleasure.

And even as Tallie battled a sense of jealousy for that position against the big man's shoulder, his powerful hand gentle on the tiny back, she knew Andrew had just taken a step toward winning over Ry and she was glad to see it.

"I better get out of here," she said.

But before she'd moved, Ry stalled her with an ornery smile that seeped through her pores. "You might want to take the Band-Aid off your forehead first," he said, barely suppressing laughter at her now, much the way she'd been doing with him.

But she wasn't embarrassed. Instead she basked in the teasing light coming from his eyes and pulled the Band-Aid off.

Then she forced herself to move from the headiness of being that near to Ry and gathered everything back into her carryall. She slung it over one shoulder, reminding Buzz to do the exercises he was assigned between the visits she no longer made every day and telling Ry she'd see him shortly before seven.

Then, as usual, she saw herself to the front door.

But not without those same heart palpitations she seemed to develop every time she got anywhere around Ry.

Even as she told herself firmly that no matter how sexy he was, not matter how gorgeous he was, she didn't want anything to do with him on any kind of personal level.

Then she spent the whole drive back into Elk Creek trying to believe it.

Chapter Two

Within an hour after Tallie had left, Ry had followed all her instructions. He'd moved a bed in one of the guest rooms into the position she'd told him to, surrounding it with kitchen chairs.

He'd given the little boy some juice—Andrew had refused to drink milk at any temperature—and done an unskilled, inept diaper change on the squirming child. Then Andrew had watched Ry suspiciously as Ry took off the tiny tennis shoes, and kept up that sober stare-down as Ry put him in bed and left the room. Ten minutes after that, when Ry peeked in again, the tiny tot was sound asleep.

And Ry was as relieved as he would have been to find himself with no broken bones after being thrown from a wild stallion.

Free of the baby, Ry used the opportunity to shower the travel dust off and then sat on the edge of his bed towel-drying his hair and thinking about the whirlwind that had swept through his life in the past week. Worse than a whirl-wind. A full-blown tornado.

He felt shell-shocked.

And none of what he'd learned, none of what had happened, seemed real.

Shelly and Dirk dead...

He still couldn't grasp that. Or why, every time he reminded himself that it was true, he felt so bad.

He didn't think it should have had such a powerful effect on him. After all, they'd stopped meaning anything to him almost three years ago.

At least they'd stopped meaning anything good to him almost three years ago.

But even if what they'd come to mean to him since then was all bad, he hadn't wanted them dead. As angry, as hurt, as disillusioned, as thunderstruck as he'd felt since that ugly day he'd had his eyes opened, he still hadn't wished anything like this on them.

Or anything like fathering their son himself after the fact, either.

Fathering their son...

Fathering? He was a father?

Lord. Somehow he hadn't thought of it like that. Guardian—that's how everyone he'd dealt with in the past week had referred to him. He'd been named Andrew's guardian. But he was going to raise the boy. And the man who raised him would be his father, one way or another.

His *father*...

Ry suffered a wave of pure fear the likes of which he couldn't remember feeling since he wasn't much older than Andrew himself.

He wasn't ready to be a father; that's all there was to it. Sure, he wanted kids—a son—someday. But not yet. Not on his own. Not by default. Definitely not without warning.

And there hadn't been any warning, damn Dirk and Shelly anyway.

Ry couldn't fathom how his former friend and the woman Ry had loved could have willed him that boy without so much as asking first if he was willing to raise him. To be a *father* to him.

But then Shelly wasn't known for doing things the right way, was she? And why not use Ry for this? It wasn't as if she hadn't used him for her own purposes before.

Damn, if thinking about it all again couldn't clench him up inside.

And double damn his own wandering thoughts that kept him looking at Andrew and thinking that, under other circumstances, the boy might really have been his....

Ry put more force into toweling his hair, as if that would rub away all that was in his mind, tormenting him.

No sense going over any of the past now. Andrew *was* his. Like it or not. Ready or not...

A soft knock on his door brought Ry's head out from under the towel as he called a quiet "Come in." Then he stood and went to his closet for a clean shirt.

He knew who his visitor was without looking. Now that Buzz was using a walker, the old man was getting around well. And Ry had no doubts his grandfather had questions for him.

"Boy sleepin'?" Buzz said in lieu of a greeting.

"Yep."

"Good. Is it the truth what you said when you got home? You're his guardian?"

"Yep."

"Sure yer not his daddy?"

"Yep." Ry shrugged into a bright yellow shirt with a red-and-black Indian design embroidered in the Western points of the yoke that saddled each shoulder, vaguely wondering at his own choice since it was not an everyday shirt, but one he saved for special occasions.

"How'd this all happen?" Buzz asked.

"You know as much as I do. I didn't even know Dirk had a kid, let alone that he'd named me guardian of it if something happened to both him and Shelly—"

"Shelly's the one, isn't she? The one who tore

yer heart out and stomped all over it. Shane told me 'bout that."

Ry didn't comment. Instead he said, "I called Maya and Shane as soon as I got to Cheyenne—I knew where they were staying for their honeymoon even though they kept it a secret from everybody else. Shane told me in case something happened around here and I needed to get hold of him. I don't suppose it ever occurred to him that I'd show up."

"What'd you need 'em for?"

"The boy went into foster care after the accident because there wasn't any family to take him in. The state was dealing with him and the will that named me as the person who inherited him. They weren't going to just hand him over to me—you know as well as I do what happens when the authorities step in."

"Humph! I remember how they had to put everybody under a microscope to see if you were fit to have *me* move in here," Buzz grumbled.

"Well, the same things applied with the boy. And since Maya hasn't formally resigned from being a caseworker for social services yet, I figured she was the best person to walk me through it all. She pulled a few strings to hurry things along. It helped that there was a recent home study done on us. Since we qualified to care for an ornery old cuss like you, we also qualified for takin' in that boy. Responsible, reliable, decent, moral and law-abiding—that's how she wrote us up. There was no question that I could support the child and provide a good environment, so I passed muster and here we are."

"Don't seem too happy 'bout it."

"It's been a long week. And the whole thing is...so unexpected. I'll get used to it."

"There's a lot to raisin' a child," Buzz cautioned.

"Yep," Ry agreed, not letting his grandfather see just how that was weighing on him.

"Think you can handle it?" the elderly man asked.

"Guess I'll have to, won't I? Hopefully Tallie will be able to whip me into shape."

That made Buzz chuckle. "If anybody can do it, she can. And you just might enjoy the process," he added slyly as he backed out of the doorway, apparently satisfied for the moment and obviously amused by the idea of Tallie whipping someone besides him into shape for a change.

But all Ry could think of as he took a pair of fresh jeans from his bureau was that, at that moment, Tallie Shanahan seemed like a lifeline to him. If anyone could turn a weather-worn bachelor like him into at least a passable parent, it was Tallie.

After all, from what he'd seen of her since Buzz had returned to the ranch, she could do just about anything. Hadn't she gotten the cantankerous, stubborn old mule back on his feet in no time? Didn't she come in here every day like a ray of sunshine and brighten up the whole place even as she took charge? Didn't she have a voice that could make a command sound like music to the ears and leave a man willing to jump through hoops to please her?

"Whoa…" he said to himself, realizing he was getting carried away if he was thinking about jumping through hoops to please anybody.

But deep down he still knew it was true.

He didn't want to admit it, but it was.

There was something about her that had him sitting up and taking notice; that was for sure. Even though he'd been trying not to.

She was just downright adorable. Fresh faced. Flawless, as far as he was concerned.

He liked that pure, porcelain skin she had. It made his fingers itch to feel it, to learn if it was as smooth and soft as it appeared to be.

Her hair was the color of white chocolate. White chocolate curls that were never really tame. He liked that, too. And the way it fell over one side of her forehead in a small cascade. Shiny, silky. Happy looking. That was it, she had happy hair.

And she had the damned cutest nose, too. Small and turned up at the end. Plus incredible eyes beneath long, thick lashes. Huge blue eyes that sparkled with life, with energy, with a secret kind of delight deep inside that made him want to know what she was thinking to cause it all.

She had a great mouth, too. Slightly wide, with a thin, dainty upper lip and a fuller, lush lower one that he kept imagining himself nibbling...

Nibbling while he held her in his arms. Discovering for himself that she felt as feminine as she looked, a mixture of soft and firm, of gentle curves and intriguing hollows. He imagined making her come alive with the sensuality he could see waiting beneath the surface. He could almost feel her moving in response to his touch, writhing just a bit, her smallish breasts against his chest, in his hands....

Ry took a deep pull of air and snapped himself out of his reverie, mentally taking himself to task as he grabbed a pair of jeans from a dresser drawer and yanked them on with a vengeance born of self-disgust.

Okay, so he was doing more than taking notice of her. He was having a lot of trouble staying out of some pretty vivid fantasies of her, too.

Not that he hadn't worked at it, because he had.

Tallie was a hometown girl, and her return to Elk Creek had set tongues wagging. Rumor had it that she and her high-school sweetheart had a notorious on-again, off-again relationship that she'd just fled in the most recent off-again phase. A relationship no one doubted would be on-again as soon as her old flame got around to coming for her.

Ry hadn't lived in Elk Creek when Tallie originally had so he hadn't seen for himself any of what folks were gossiping about. But he had to take seriously talk like that, from people who knew her when.

The fact of the matter was, there was another man in her life.

Much the way there had been another man in Shelly's life.

And that was a great big glaring red light to Ry.

A great big glaring red light that was reason enough for him to keep his distance. At least as much as he could with her at the house nearly every day working with Buzz.

Unfortunately that red light and the distance hadn't been able to keep his mind from wandering to Tallie with a will of its own. Like just now. And way too often to leave him comfortable.

Still, he'd managed to keep things cool. On

the surface, anyway. He hadn't asked her out. He hadn't let anything but Buzz's health and well-being be the topic of conversation between them. He'd ignored the fact that just knowing what time of day she'd be showing up at the ranch would cause excitement to build in him as that time approached. And he'd told himself that the sooner Buzz's therapy was finished the better so he wouldn't be seeing Tallie except on the street or at town functions and could finally shake whatever it was about her that seemed to have infected him.

"Only now she'll be takin' a hand with me," he muttered to himself, feeling a dangerous thrill rush through him as a more literal image of her taking a hand with him flashed through his mind.

All right. So a part of him was all worked up by the idea of getting to spend some one-on-one time with her. Some time all his own.

But it wasn't the sane, rational part of him, the part that had learned the harsh lesson Shelly had taught him.

And the sane, rational part of him was no weak willy. With the exception of that brief lapse with Shelly, it had kept him in check for thirty-seven years. It could keep him in check now. He'd make sure of it.

Because even if his life wasn't in a total uproar, even if he was willing to take a risk on a relationship again, it wouldn't be with a woman who had any ties whatsoever to another man.

It was just a good thing he was a fast learner, he told himself as he tucked his shirt into his jeans. He'd absorb all he needed to know and then he'd redouble his efforts to keep his distance from Tallie. No matter how cute she was. How nice. How sweet. How subtly sexy. No matter how attracted he might be to her. No matter how many fantasies crept into his head.

He wasn't interested in the tender trap of an appealing woman who wasn't as free as she seemed to be.

Because that tender trap had treacherous jaws.

Jaws that could clamp down when he wasn't looking.

And take a bite out of his heart…

TALLIE HAD TO really rush to get to the baby shop before seven. It was her own fault. Her last appointment of the day had been a case of athlete's foot at six. Then she'd had to close up the office. If she'd gone straight to the store after closing, she would have made it on time. But she hadn't done that.

Instead she'd gone home to change her clothes.

She'd told herself it was because she'd been wearing what she had on since 5:00 a.m. That the clothes were wrinkled. That she didn't want to spend her evening in the slacks and blouse that were work garb, and that after a long day she deserved to get more comfortable.

That didn't, however, cover the fact that she'd refreshed her makeup and redone her hair. Or the fact that the *more comfortable* clothes she'd changed into were her tightest pair of jeans and a scoop-necked T-shirt so snug it fit like sausage casing.

Date clothes were what they were.

Not that she had any illusions that the evening she was about to spend with Ry was a date. But somehow, when she'd stared into her closet, those were just the clothes she'd been driven to wear.

She swore to herself as she turned onto Center Street—Elk Creek's main thoroughfare—that she would keep everything in perspective from there on, though.

Of course it didn't occur to her as she raced down the extrawide avenue that her every sense was tuned to spotting Ry rather than to so much as noticing any of the quaint, well-tended, mostly Victorian-style stores and businesses that lined both sides of the street.

The baby shop was in the middle of the block,

a double storefront with maternity clothes on one side and everything a baby or small child could ever need on the other.

It was on that second side that Tallie parked—nose to the curb. She spotted Ry just inside the door that was recessed between two glass cantilevered display windows and got out of her sedan in such a hurry once she'd turned off the engine that she left her keys in the ignition. She barely heard the irritating buzz that reminded her of it and didn't stop long enough to remove them even then.

"Sorry I'm late. My last appointment ran over," she lied, as if her obvious change of clothes wouldn't give her away.

But before Ry could comment on that, she added, "I hope Bitsy doesn't mind if we keep her open a little late. Did you explain to her what's going on?"

"Told her I needed to be outfitted for my new station in life as a parent. She offered to be my personal shopper, but I told her I had you for that job so she left us a salesgirl and a stock boy and went home."

Tallie had known and liked Bitsy Newkirk all her life. But she still felt a surge of relief at hearing Bitsy had gone home. Bitsy was thirty-eight, still single and would like nothing better than to be the handsome Ry's personal anything. Tallie was just glad the other woman had left.

"Well, here I am," Tallie said, watching Ry juggle Andrew.

The big man and the little boy were doing an odd kind of dance as Andrew alternately squirmed to get down and tried to climb Ry's body like a monkey on a tree. Ry countered by switching Andrew awkwardly from one hip to the other and back several times before he resorted to carrying the child at his side like a saddle again. That defeated Andrew's attempts to get a foot- or a handhold, so he wiggled and put up a fuss.

The sight helped Tallie forget about her competition and made her smile. It was funny to see a man like Ry, who could master everything else, being done in by a small child.

"Why don't we get a shopping buggy and put him in that?" she suggested, pulling one from a row of the grocery-store-like carts.

She pushed the seat open and showed Ry how to get the wriggling child's legs through the openings to set him in it.

Andrew offered a loud but brief protest—letting it be known he would have preferred to have the run of the store—but was easily distracted by a box of animal crackers Tallie had brought for just that purpose.

With the child finally placated, Ry breathed a sigh of relief that Tallie didn't think she was supposed to hear. She had to laugh at him.

"Better?" she asked, teasing him.

He gave her a stern frown that was belied by the chagrined half smile he also threw her way. "Boy's a handful," he said as if relief was what anybody would feel after dealing with the imp.

A knowing "Mmm" was all Tallie answered, feasting on the disarmingly attractive sight of Ry in jeans and a dressy yellow shirt that brought out the highlights in his hair. She had to wonder if she was mistaken or if he might have spruced up a bit for her tonight, too.

"Are you ready for this?" she asked.

That made him laugh, a rich, throaty sound she'd never heard before that sent a warm wave of pleasure through her.

"I don't think I can wait till I'm ready. Let's just do it."

Shopping was not what skipped through her mind in terms of *doing it,* but she shooed the unwarranted titillation away and said, "Call in the troops."

Two teenagers joined them then, the stock boy pushing another buggy and the salesgirl keeping a running tab as they swept through the place.

It was fun shopping with a man who had no

budget or qualms about spending money. Every-thing Tallie pointed out—from bare necessities to toys and bedtime storybooks—Ry instructed the stock boy to take off the shelves.

The largest purchase was a twin-size bed that came equipped with rails all around to prevent the child from rolling out of it. Neither the bed nor the rails were high off the ground, so Andrew could easily climb over them without being hurt. And once he was past the stage of falling out of bed, the rails could be removed.

It cost Ry more and required a phone call to Bitsy for an okay, but he managed to buy the already assembled display model, which he and the stock boy maneuvered out of the store with some difficulty and loaded onto the rear of Ry's tan truck once he'd paid for everything.

To secure the bed, Ry took a long rope from behind the seat, spun it expertly over his head until he had a large, even loop twirling there. Then he sent it flying through the air to where it caught a high point on the headboard. A hearty yank tightened the noose, a few more turns, loops and pulls and a finishing knot, and he had the bed trussed up as good and tight as any steer ready for a branding.

The exhibition made Tallie laugh again. The man carried the baby like a saddle and lassoed the bed. He was clearly more suited to being out on the range than to playing daddy.

"What?" he asked as he hopped down from the truck to land in front of her on the curb where she stood holding Andrew.

"You're not fumble fingered with that, are you?" she observed with a nod toward the rope, also noticing as he stood so nearby just how tall and broad shouldered he was.

He held his hands out, palms up, glanced down at them and then up at Tallie as he flexed them into big, brawny fists and opened them again. "I'm not fumble fingered with anything but that boy there," he said with a sexy lift to one eyebrow that made his comment seem like an innuendo.

But then it occurred to Tallie that she might just be reading more into things than he intended because something about those powerful, masculine hands with their long, thick fingers set off twitterings in the pit of her stomach…and lower…as she wondered out of the blue what they might feel like on her body.

And fumble fingered was *not* part of the image her mind conjured up in answer.…

She cleared her throat when what she really needed was to clear her mind. "I'll put in the car seat while you load the rest," she offered then, deciding it was better if she wasn't just standing there watching Ry.

Andrew was only too willing to be set on the truck's bench seat on the driver's side while Tallie situated the safety seat. The little boy sat up as tall as he could on his knees so he could reach the steering wheel, pretending he was driving and even making a noise vaguely like an engine.

As Tallie faced the rear of the truck cab to fasten the baby carrier with seat belts, she couldn't help looking out the back window. Directly at Ry's derriere where he'd positioned himself beside the bed to catch all the packages the stock boy tossed up to him.

Off went the internal twitterings all over again as Tallie's gaze glued itself to the finest buns she thought she'd ever seen cupped in a pair of blue jeans. Not to mention the finest legs with thighs so thick they stretched the denim to its limits, and a narrow waist that did a slow rise into wide, hard-muscled shoulders.

So much for distracting herself.

Tallie couldn't tear her eyes away. Instead she stayed frozen to the spot, her own weight braced on both hands on the arms of the baby seat, gawking like a child at its first Christmas tree.

But oh, what a man he was! A tall, lean mass of arousing masculinity.

"Do you need help?"

It took Tallie longer than it should have to realize that question came from the salesgirl and was directed at her.

When it finally sank in, she jolted up. Too far up. She hit her head on the cab's roof with a thud loud enough to stop Ry and make him ask if she was all right.

One more glance out the rear window, and Tallie realized what she was looking at was even worse than what she'd been drawn to before. Because now that he'd turned in her direction, she was staring out at the bulging zipper of his jeans.

Her mouth went dry, her mind went blank and her body turned to 110 pounds of mush.

"Fine," she managed to squeak out. "I'm fine," she added to include the salesgirl.

"Boo-boo?" Andrew asked.

"Just a little one," Tallie confirmed.

The baby walked on his knees to her, grasped her face in both his hands, pulled it down and kissed the top of her head.

That made her and everyone else laugh and helped ease Tallie out of the embarrassment she'd caused herself.

"Come on, you little sweetheart," she said to the baby, lifting him into his car seat and pulling down the belts that slipped over his head to fasten between his chubby legs.

"We're all set," Ry called from outside.

Tallie looked up in time to see him vault over the side of the truck in one lithe leap any gymnast would have been proud of.

"We're all set, too," she answered.

Then she moved to get out of the truck and caught Ry doing some ogling of his own. At her derriere.

The expression on his handsome face said he was enjoying the view, and Tallie felt way more pleased by that than she wanted to.

Pleased enough to take her time getting out of the truck.

"Is there any chance I could convince you to come home with me now and show me what to do with all this stuff?" he asked in a voice that sounded even more husky than usual.

"I figured I'd need to," she said. It was another lie. She hadn't thought beyond their shopping trip and how to keep her own raging hormones in control. But now that it was time to either go home with him or go home alone, instructing him on how to use his new paraphernalia sounded like a good idea.

Even though she knew it shouldn't.

"I'll just follow you in my car," she said.

He smiled at her with more warmth than mere paraphernalia instruction seemed to warrant. "Terrific."

The sun had gone down on the early June night by then and since hot weather had yet to start, Tallie used the cool air like a cold shower as she drove behind the tan truck with its much too intriguing driver.

The whole way she lectured herself about getting some control, thinking that she should have used the time after closing up her office tonight to eat something rather than to change her clothes. Maybe lack of food was making her weak willed. Maybe not enough sugar in her blood had left her vulnerable to something else in it—like an ever growing attraction to Ry.

But enough was enough, she told herself. She had to get a grip.

And she was determined to do just that.

Right up to the moment she parked her car in front of the McDermot house and watched Ry back his truck onto the lawn and walkway that led to the front door.

He had one arm stretched across the top of the seat, his long, thick neck craned so he could see what he was doing, his sculptured features in profile to her and glazed golden by the bright lantern lights just under the eaves. She could feel herself weaken with the sight.

She'd been vulnerable to this man since meeting him the first day she'd come to work with Buzz. But spending time with him one-on-

one tonight had made it much worse. She decided that if she couldn't control it she'd better pitch in, help get the truck unloaded, do her instructing and get out of there as soon as possible. Maybe some food and a good night's sleep would dilute the potency of his effect on her and she'd be better able to resist the attraction.

Andrew had fallen asleep on the short ride home, and as Ry went in search of ranch hands to help with the bed, Tallie released the car seat and carried the baby carefully inside so as not to wake him.

Once she got there she decided that she'd speed things up by undressing him and putting on his pajamas while Ry and the other men got the bed in.

The whole while they did that, she worked hard at gently caring for Andrew and not watching the play of muscles it took for Ry to move the bed.

He made up the bed in a hurry after he and his assistants had it situated in the sitting room connected to his bedroom, and before Tallie knew it the still sleeping baby was tucked in.

And she was alone with Ry.

"Where's Buzz tonight?" she asked as Ry led the way into the living room where the ranch hands had brought in all the rest of the things already.

"One of his cronies picked him up to play poker."

Which meant they really were alone....

"Can I get you somethin' to drink? Iced tea? Wine?"

"No. Thanks. I'm fine," she lied for the third time, reminding herself not to prolong this any more than necessary. "Shall we get through lesson number one on this stuff?" she asked with a nod toward all the packages. "I thought I'd just go through enough to get you started and then let you relax. I imagine you're about done in by now—what with traveling this morning and everything with Andrew since then. It's probably been a long day for you."

"It has," he agreed. "But I'm feelin' pretty relaxed."

Well, she wasn't—that was for sure. As her grandmother used to say, she was as nervous as a long-tailed cat in a room full of rocking chairs.

And the best way to get through it was to get down to business. So that's what she opted to do.

She unwrapped the sippy cups from their packaging and told him to make sure he washed them before he used them, also instructing Ry to offer Andrew milk, juice and water periodically, not just with meals.

After mentioning that he should also wash the toddler's rubber-coated silverware, she made sure to tell him to cut all the child's food into very small bites and what foods—like hot dogs—could actually be dangerous for him to eat.

She told Ry what to do with Andrew if he woke in the middle of the night, advising against bringing him into Ry's bed. She told him not to be surprised if the baby was up with the roosters at the crack of dawn, or alarmed if he slept till nine or ten.

She talked about cutting Andrew's fingernails with the baby nail clippers she'd had him buy when she'd noticed how long the child's nails were, about trying to get Andrew to blow his nose since he seemed to have some congestion and about how to use the nasal aspirator if he couldn't get Andrew to do it the easy way.

She cautioned him to double-knot the laces on the child's tennis shoes and to be ever watchful if he took Andrew outside with him to work— telling him that a nineteen-month-old baby could get into more mischief in ten minutes than Ry would ever guess.

Tallie explained why the tiny jeans that he'd bought, with the snaps down the inside of each leg, were so convenient and showed him how to do a diaper change with them. She also gave him a refresher course in the diapers themselves since she'd discovered Andrew's to be much too loose when she'd gotten him ready for bed.

She advised Ry to use the sun screen she'd had him buy, she showed him how to operate the high chair and the bath towel with the hooded corner, and together they figured out where to put the bubble solution in the toy lawnmower he'd thought Andrew would get a kick out of.

Then, intent on showing him what to do with the car seat on her way out, she headed back to the truck that was still parked just outside the house.

Ry opened the passenger's door and set the seat inside.

Tallie had to climb into the cab again to show him how to secure and release it and what to do with Andrew to get him in and out of it.

As she did, Ry leaned inside with her, close enough for her to smell the faint lingering of after-shave.

It made her voice crack and renewed what she thought she'd conquered once she'd gotten into the swing of teaching him—a heightened awareness of the man himself.

Good time to go home, she thought.

"Okay. I think you have the hang of it," she

said with too much cheerfulness when it seemed he could fasten and unfasten all the belts in all the right places.

He agreed and moved out of the way so she could get down from the truck.

But in her hurry to do that, she stood up straighter than she should have and again hit her head on the cab roof.

"Ow…" she groaned as she rubbed it on the way out. "I think you need higher ceilings in there."

When her feet hit the ground, she glanced up at Ry and found him trying to keep from laughing. "Boo-boo?" he asked, mimicking Andrew's earlier question. Except that he managed to make even the baby talk sound sensual.

Then, before Tallie knew what he was up to, he reached over, cupped both sides of her face in his hands and tipped it downward so he could kiss her head just as Andrew had.

It was only a joke, she kept telling herself. Ry was merely kidding around.

But still, it was the first time he'd ever touched her. And she was much, much too aware of the feel of those callused hands against her cheeks, of the heated press of his lips to her head, of the hot honey that sluiced all through her in response.

And of a strong, strong urge to raise her face and meet those lips with her own...

"Gee, thanks," she managed to say a split second later when he let her go, in keeping with the less serious tone she was certain he intended.

"Just glad to get my turn," he answered, sounding only half-teasing.

Tallie looked up into his heart-stoppingly handsome face, bathed once more in lamplight, and couldn't tell how much of what had just passed between them really was simply in fun and how much might have had more meaning.

Or maybe she was just indulging in wishful thinking.

Either way, it wasn't good.

"Well, that concludes tonight's lesson," she said then, purposely sounding like an announcer on instructional television.

Ry continued to stare at her a moment longer before he nodded an agreement and stepped back to give her some breathing room. "Thanks for everything," he said, sounding like himself again—free of innuendo and sensuality.

And she was suddenly disappointed to lose that brief glimpse of the lighter side of him. The very appealing, sexy lighter side.

But what could she do about it? What *should* she do about it?

She should be glad and leave—that's what.

"I'm happy to help," she said in answer to his thanks. Then she headed for her car.

Ry came along and she didn't know what else to say, so she stated, "Remember that my parenting class is tomorrow night. I'm going over childproofing the home."

"Is that where I'll learn what to do with all those cupboard and corner protector doohickeys you had me buy?"

"Among other things."

"Then I'll be there. Seven-thirty, right?"

"Right."

They'd reached her car by then, and he opened the driver's-side door for her.

"I really do appreciate this. I'm gonna have to think of somethin' pretty good to repay you."

Tallie thought of something pretty good, but it wasn't anything she could ever let him know about. Especially since it involved more of that kissing he'd only toyed with before.

She got behind the wheel and started the engine. "See you tomorrow night," she said a bit more breathlessly than she liked.

"Tomorrow night," he confirmed, stepping away from the car but not going any farther, staying to watch her as she finally pulled away from the curb and headed down his private drive.

That was when she yanked herself back to reality and reminded herself that there was nothing going on between her and Ry McDermot. That this was *not* the start of some kind of romance and that she'd just better get those wandering thoughts of hers in line.

Because if she didn't, she was setting herself up for the same sort of fall she'd suffered over and over again with Justin. The kind of fall that came from giving in to hopes and dreams and unreal expectations rather than seeing things—and people—the way they really were.

"You came back to Elk Creek to keep your feet firmly planted on the ground. To live in the real world," she said firmly.

And in the real world, Ry McDermot had not given her the time of day until now, when he needed her services, and that kiss he'd planted on the top of her head had been nothing more than a joke.

The truth was that there was nothing between them but a passing acquaintance and that was all there ever *would* be between them. All she ever *wanted* there to be between them.

She had herself convinced of it as she pulled into her driveway.

Or at least she thought she did.

Until she slipped into her bed an hour later, closed her eyes and discovered the image of ranch-made muscles and those gorgeous green eyes right there in her mind again.

And an odd craving to let that image have its effect on the rest of her body…

Chapter Three

As usual the next day was a hectic one for Tallie. She had appointments until six that she didn't actually finish until seven. Her parenting class was scheduled for seven-thirty, so she again had the choice of getting something to eat or changing her clothes and fixing her hair and makeup.

Ordinarily she opted for making a quick dash to the Dairy King for a burger before her Tuesday and Thursday sessions. But tonight—like the previous one—she ignored her hunger pangs and made a quick dash home to spruce up.

She was aggravated with herself as she hurried to the small white frame house that she'd grown up in and taken over from her family when her father had passed away and her mother had decided to move into a retirement community in Cheyenne. She was aggravated with herself as she hurried to shed her work clothes and put on her black cat suit and the brightly colored swing vest she wore over it. She was aggravated with herself the whole time she was reapplying mascara, blush and a new lipstick she'd bought. She was aggravated with herself the whole time she was brushing her hair and fluffing the curls with her fingers.

She was aggravated with herself because there was only one reason she was doing any of that.

And that reason was Ry McDermot.

She hadn't come back to her hometown to hook up with a man to replace Justin. She'd come to get away from Justin. To start over *without* a man in her life at all.

It hadn't occurred to her that the small town she'd always thought she knew inside and out might have a few new citizens who would be so incredibly good-looking, so incredibly appealing, so incredibly sexy, that she'd be irresistibly drawn to one of them.

Irresistibly and unwillingly.

She honestly didn't want to be entangled with another man right now. After being involved with Justin Wendt since she was a teenager, she'd decided it was high time she spent some time on her own. Doing her own thing. Doing as she pleased, when she pleased, where she pleased, how she pleased. Exploring the joys of singlehood.

Okay, so she hadn't found too much joy in any of that. And doing her own thing, doing as she pleased, when she pleased, where she pleased, how she pleased, got boring after a while. Not to mention lonely.

But even so, even if she was longing for a little company—a little *male* company—she ought to know better than to pick someone like Ry.

What was wrong with her? she asked herself. Was it the challenge of an aloof man that reached out to some psychological need in her? A man who was remote? Who seemed just out of reach? A man like Justin who held just enough of himself in escrow to never really commit to a relationship?

How many disappointments did she need in her life? Hadn't Justin provided enough to last forever? How could she be hung up on another man who wasn't wholeheartedly enamored with her?

Hung up?

That phrase slowed her down some in her rush to gather her soiled clothes and stuff them into the hamper.

Was she hung up on Ry?

She hoped not.

But she was afraid it was coming to that. Try as she might to keep it from happening.

And as for his being wholeheartedly enamored? She couldn't even say he was slightly interested.

Well, maybe slightly.

There had been that kiss after she'd bumped her head the second time the previous night.

But that had only been a joke, she reminded herself for what seemed like the millionth time since it had happened.

Of course he hadn't ever joked with her before. And there had been a glint of something in his eyes....

Hadn't there?

Or was she just projecting what she wanted to see in them?

Could he honestly have been flirting...even just a bit...with her?

"Don't think about that!" she told her reflection in the mirror as she took one last check on her appearance before she raced out of the house.

But she was still thinking about the possibility that Ry had been flirting with her—just a little—all the way back to the old Molner Mansion, which served as Elk Creek's medical facility.

She was thinking about the possibility that he'd been flirting with her and she was also thinking about the feel of his hands on her skin. Of that moment when his lips had touched her head. Of how he'd smelled—clean and just slightly citrusy. Of the warmth that had radiated from his big body right into hers. Of how much she'd wanted him to kiss her lips instead...

Maybe she was just a glutton for punishment, she told herself. Why else would she be indulging in these thoughts, these fantasies, these hopes, when she knew darned good and well nothing was going to come of them?

"So enough!" she ordered herself as she rushed to the meeting room on the second floor of the mansion where she held her class.

And she meant it, too.

She'd had enough of unmet hopes and dreams and she was not going to risk having any more of them. That's why she'd come home to Elk Creek. That's what she intended to hold on to. By hook or by crook.

Except that when she turned on the lights to the meeting room, the first thing she did was look up at the schoolhouse clock on the wall and wish that Ry would arrive early. Before anyone else got there. So she could have a few minutes alone with him.

Maybe she really *was* a glutton for punishment.

Actually she was convinced of it when the sound of the meeting room's door opening behind her five minutes later gave her the thrill of her life.

Unfortunately, when she turned around, it was Kansas Daye...Kansas Heller now...who walked in.

Not that Tallie wasn't glad to see Kansas. Tallie, Kansas and Maya Wilson—who had just married Ry's twin brother, Shane—had been best friends all through their growing-up years in Elk Creek. They'd been inseparable. They'd stayed in touch even after Tallie and Maya had left town, and now that they were back, the friendship had picked up right where it had left off.

But still Tallie felt a wave of disappointment. Not at who her first arrival was. But at who it wasn't.

It wasn't Ry.

"Hi! You're early," Tallie said, forcing a cheerfulness she didn't fully feel.

"I never get to see you these days, you're so busy. Linc can't make class tonight—he has a lot of staff out sick over at the honky tonk and he had to work. So I thought, since I was coming alone, I'd come a little ahead of time and say hey."

"Well, hey," Tallie joked.

"Hey yourself," Kansas joked back.

The room was large, and a long oval conference table took up the entire center, surrounded by sixteen high-backed chairs. Tallie stood at the head, setting out the visual aids for her childproofing-the-home lecture.

"Have you heard anything about your baby?" she asked then.

Kansas pulled out the chair to Tallie's right and sat down. She was stepmother to Linc Heller's young son, Danny, but the medical necessity of an early hysterectomy had left her unable to have kids of her own. She and her husband, Linc, had put in for adoption and were now awaiting the birth of the baby girl they were going to get.

"All's well," Kansas answered Tallie's question. "Our due date is in two weeks, and we have dibs on Jackson and his helicopter so the minute labor starts he can fly us to Casper for the birth."

"And you'll get to take the baby home straight from the hospital?"

"That's the plan. I can't wait! We're so excited at our house right now that none of us are hardly sleeping."

Tallie reached out a hand to squeeze one of Kansas's. "I'm so happy for you. You deserve this." Then she let go and laughed. "But you'd better get some sleep now because once that baby is here…"

Victoria Pade   63

"I know, I know. But I'm even anxious for 2:00 a.m. feedings."

"Guess I'm not the only one who's a glutton for punishment," Tallie said half under her breath.

"What does that mean? How are you a glutton for punishment?" Kansas asked. Then, as if she'd come up with her own answer, she said, "How are things going with you? Have you heard from Justin yet?"

Tallie opted for ignoring that second query and only answering the first. "I'm fine. Busy. I'll be glad when the committee decides who they're going to hire as the new doctor so I can ease up some, but other than that—"

"And Justin?" her friend persisted. "Have you heard from him?"

Tallie's former flame had also grown up in Elk Creek and gone to school with the rest of them, so Kansas knew him. She also knew most of Tallie's history with him.

"No," Tallie said simply. "I haven't heard from him."

"You will."

"It's over between us, Kansas."

Kansas laughed. "How many times have I heard that? A hundred?"

"I mean it."

"And that I've heard at least ninety-nine

times. I don't believe it, and neither does anybody else who knows you. You and Justin always do this. You break up. He sweet-talks you and you go back. You've been doing it since we were all kids."

"We're not kids anymore. Maybe I've finally learned my lesson."

"You and Justin belong together."

"I used to think so, too."

"But you don't anymore," Kansas said skeptically.

"Now I think maybe the whole thing just ran its course."

"That was some kind of long course. You've been goo-goo-eyed over Justin Wendt since we were thirteen."

"And that was long enough."

Kansas looked surprised and changed her tone. "You almost sound serious. Did he do something horrible this time?"

"It's always the same old story, Kansas—he promises tomorrow but tomorrow never comes. Only I'm not the same old girl anymore."

"Oh, you don't mean that."

The meeting room door opened again, and Tallie's glance shot there all on its own.

But once she saw that it was only the janitor, poking his head in to confirm that she was using the room tonight, she deflated a little.

Though not so little that Kansas didn't pick up on it.

"There's someone else, isn't there?"

"If there was, Justin didn't let on," Tallie said, purposely misinterpreting her friend.

"I don't mean there's someone else with Justin—I mean there's someone else for you."

"No, of course there isn't."

Kansas paid no attention to that. "Maya was right. She told me she thought you had a thing for Ry McDermot. And now that he's inherited that baby, I'll bet he's coming to these classes to learn what to do with it. That's who you were hoping was coming through that door just now, isn't it?"

Tallie rolled her eyes but couldn't suppress a smile at her old friend's accuracy even as she denied that Kansas had hit the nail on the head.

"So Justin finally has some competition," Kansas concluded.

"You have this all wrong."

"Ha! Does he know?"

"Nobody knows anything because there isn't anything to know."

But that didn't convince Kansas any more than the rest of what Tallie had said. Tallie knew her friend could see right through her and even though the other members of the class began arriving, Kansas sat where she was with a smug, knowing expression on her face.

THERE WAS A baby boom in Elk Creek.

Besides Kansas and the absent Linc Heller, the Heller clan had had a very fertile year. Linc's brother, Jackson, and his wife, Ally, were a part of Tallie's class, too. Ally already had a nine-year-old daughter—Meggie—but as Ally had explained, nine years was a long time between babies and a lot of things had changed. There were new gadgets and improvements on old ones, and she wanted an update on the latest in babyland to prepare her for her and Jackson's impending bundle of joy. Plus Jackson was a first-time father so he felt he needed the education.

Linc and Jackson's sister, Beth, and her husband, Ash Blackwolf, also attended. Beth was pregnant with their second child even though their first was only a year old. A lot of what Tallie had to say was repetitious for them, but they were patient with her while awaiting the portion of the class that would deal with potty training, the terrible twos and more of the things that applied to parents of a soon-to-be toddler.

The Hellers' cousin Ivey and her husband, Clint Culhane, were also expecting, as were Kansas's sister Della and her husband Yance—

Cully's brother. Della and Yance took the most teasing since Della had apparently gotten pregnant on her honeymoon. And like Jackson and Ally, even though Della was an old hand with babies—having four of her own kids with her late first husband—Yance was a rookie in search of training for what was to come.

Rounding out the group was Hope Davidson, whose husband was in Australia on business. She'd roped her sister Carly into coming to the classes with her because some minor complications had left her unable to drive herself. There wasn't much Tallie could teach Hope that she didn't already know as the mother of three, but in a small town like Elk Creek just about any get-together was a draw. For Hope it was an excuse to get a baby-sitter and have a night out.

Hope and Carly arrived at 7:35, completing the regular group. Carly was scheduled to leave town on a worldwide trip she'd been planning—and canceling—for what seemed like her whole life. It was the basis for some good-natured teasing about whether or not she'd really make it this time.

Ordinarily Tallie would have cut that short and launched into the evening's lecture. But tonight she let the chatter go on and on. It gave her the chance to wait. With bated breath. For Ry to show up.

In fact she waited until ten minutes to eight when Carly cried uncle and asked if Tallie was ever going to get this show on the road and rescue her.

That left Tallie without much choice but to start.

"We were supposed to have a new member tonight. I'm sure you've all heard that Ry Mc-Dermot became a parent by inheritance this week. But since it doesn't seem like he's going to make it, I guess we ought to go on without him."

And with that she felt her mood deflate and had to pretend enthusiasm she suddenly didn't have as she introduced the topic of childproofing the home.

Her heart just wasn't in cupboard locks and corner protectors. Sure, she went through the motions. She demonstrated everything she'd laid out in preparation for the class. She talked about everyday safety precautions and even a few unusual ones like alarms floating in swimming pools that warned if a child fell in when no one was looking.

And although this was commonly an enjoyable way to spend her usually empty evenings, she just couldn't get into the spirit of things.

It was an indication to her of just how much she'd been looking forward to seeing Ry tonight.

And all those dashed hopes—even if she hadn't admitted to herself that she'd been hoping for anything—served as a reminder to her.

Which was a good thing, she told herself. It was fate reopening her eyes to how rotten it was to feel let down.

But still her joy in the class never returned.

Tallie was just wrapping things up for the evening by talking about the importance of helmets for kids riding along on the back of bicycles—or horses—when the meeting-room door she'd too often glanced at finally opened.

She froze in midsentence as Ry stepped into the room like an overgrown schoolboy slightly shamefaced at his tardiness.

He was alone, and Tallie might have wondered where Andrew was if she hadn't been so intent on that initial glimpse of the new father.

Ry had on the cowboy boots that were de rigueur around those parts and blue jeans that fit every inch of long, hard legs in a loving hug. He had on a hunter green Western shirt that accentuated the color of his eyes, with the sleeves rolled to his elbows, exposing powerful forearms that—for no reason Tallie could understand—seemed terrifically sexy to her.

His hair was shiny clean and combed haphazardly away from his forehead as if by fingers, his handsome face was freshly shaved and the sheepish grin he gave her when their eyes met melted something inside her and somehow made everyone else in the room fade into the distance.

"Sorry 'bout this. I meant to be here from the start, but babies are more of a handful than I bargained for."

His apology was aimed at Tallie, but before she could think of a response everyone was congratulating him and teasing him and she'd lost her opportunity.

What was left of her lecture got lost in the shuffle from there. It was probably for the best, Tallie realized, because from the moment Ry entered the room he was too much of a distraction for her to concentrate anyway.

Instead she stayed in the background as he fended off an onslaught of questions and ribbing, and spent the whole time trying to ignore all that was stirred up in her at just the sight of him.

But it wasn't easy. Her pulse was racing; she felt reenergized, alert, alive. She lost herself in the lines that crinkled around his eyes when he laughed. In the creases that appeared down both cheeks when he smiled. In the rich mahogany of his voice. She lost all sense of time, of space, of everyone but Ry and a deep, deep wish to be alone with him.

Just when she thought she'd never be granted

that wish, Kansas noticed the late hour and stood to leave. It had a ripple effect, and couples started sending a last jab at Ry—along with an order to bring Andrew to the next session—before filing out, too.

As they did, Tallie got more and more edgy, worrying that Ry was going to leave along with one or another of them.

But he didn't.

In fact he seemed intent on lagging behind until, together, they'd bid good-night to the last of the group.

Then he stepped over to the head of the conference table and looked over Tallie's assorted props. "Bet this is all stuff I should know about."

Tallie walked up to the chair Kansas had occupied all evening and stood behind it, forcing her gaze from his face to the safety paraphernalia. "You'd win that bet."

He glanced at the clock. "Don't suppose I can persuade you to give me a quick run-through."

It was nearly ten already, and although she knew it was ridiculous, she felt as if she'd been stood up for the prom. By him. And that brought out a hint of contrariness in her. "The janitor needs to get in here and clean up so he can go home for the night. We've already kept the room overtime," she said as she leaned across the chair and began to gather her teaching aids.

"Are you peeved at me?" he asked, sounding as if it amused him.

"Of course not. Why would I be? You're the one who said you needed lessons on parenting. Your not showing up didn't stop me from giving the class. It didn't matter one way or another."

"You're peeved," he concluded.

"Don't be silly." But that had come out very huffy even though she hadn't meant for it to.

Carrying all she could manage, Tallie went to the walnut china cabinet in the corner of the room and began to put things away. She didn't know Ry had any intention of helping until he was at her side, his arms laden with the remainder of her examples of good safety.

He smelled like an orchard in the sunshine, and whether it was that or just his nearness, something made her head go light. So light she imagined herself wilting into his arms, supported against that big, rock-hard body...

"I shouldn't have skipped supper," she murmured to herself.

"Is that my fault, too?" he said with a lilt of suppressed laughter in his voice.

"As a matter of fact—" She cut herself off. "I was just thinking out loud."

"The Dairy King is probably still open. What do you say we go over and grab a burger? My treat. To make up."

Oh, great, now he probably thought she'd been fishing for a free meal. "That's okay. I only meant that I might be a little cranky because I haven't eaten since lunch."

Tallie glanced sideways to see if he was buying this load of manure.

She couldn't tell one way or another. He just seemed to be enjoying himself and her pique.

"Come on," he cajoled.

"I don't have my car. I walked here and I was going to walk home." As if that made any difference.

"The Dairy King is on the way to your place, and I've got wheels. Or we could both walk over—believe me, I could use a little winddown."

She felt like Adam being tempted by Eve in the Garden of Eden. And even though she knew no good could come of it, she heard herself say, "Okay. I have to eat."

"Oh, yeah, you're peeved," he repeated at her less than gracious acceptance, and this time Tallie felt her face flush even though his grin indicated he was still amused by her.

She closed the china cabinet and spun away from him and the heady effects he was having on her, telling herself she could do this without making a big deal of it. It wasn't a date, after all. It was just her and a fellow Elk Creekian getting a burger together. No different than if she were with any other citizen of her hometown.

Except, of course, that this particular citizen made her toes curl.

Not five minutes later they stepped from the Molner Mansion into the cool June night. Tallie took a deep breath of the clean air, hoping to exhale away the craziness that had overtaken her. The craziness that seemed to overtake her every time she was anywhere around Ry. Or even thinking about him.

Ry stretched out a long arm, pointing to the tan truck parked at the curb. "I can drive us if you want."

The idea of climbing into the cab of his truck, sitting alone with him in the confined space, set off a storm of excitement in her.

Enough of a storm to warn her.

"Walking is good," she answered, taking off at a quick pace across the manicured lawn of the medical building.

That gave her a head start, but Ry caught up in three long-legged strides that meant business as she made her way across Center Street, which circled the town square, and marched through the park lit by tall Victorian lamps amid the lofty elm, oak and fir trees.

"I didn't do it on purpose, you know," he said

when he was next to her and had slowed his pace to accommodate hers.

"Didn't do what on purpose?"

"Miss your class. I was hell-bent on comin'. Lookin' forward to it, as a matter of fact."

"Oh, sure. You were just dying to spend your evening listening about guard rails for stove tops and plugs for electrical outlets."

"What I was dyin' for was to see you," he said almost more to himself than to her, as if he didn't want to admit it.

It lit a glittery spark in Tallie that made her glance over at him as she wondered if—and maybe worried that he might be—teasing her. Just a little.

But there was no sign of it. Instead he seemed to be grappling with himself slightly.

Then he changed the subject. Or at least put it back on course. "I don't suppose I can talk you into a private tutoring session to fill me in, could I?"

She considered saying once again that she was too busy, that that was the whole purpose of his coming to the class—to get the instruction when she had time to give it since she didn't have time to provide private lessons.

But what was the point? The very idea of giving him private lessons in anything intrigued her, and she knew that she'd only come around to agreeing in the end anyway.

So, as they reached the local fast-food restaurant, she said, "I'll be at your place to do Buzz's physical therapy tomorrow afternoon. Late. If you're there, I'll go over what you missed tonight. But just this once," she warned sternly. "After this make sure you get to the class if you want to know these things."

"Yes, ma'am," he answered with a lilt to his voice that made an endearing mockery of her schoolmarmish reprimand.

The Dairy King was a white aluminum building with three half walls of windows that displayed the interior. Jutting out front and center from the building was a long concrete slab covered by a fiberglass canopy where car service was available. There was one vehicle parked there, but no one seemed to be waiting on the two teenagers in it. No other customers littered the stark inside of the place, where two more teenagers were cleaning up behind the counter.

Tallie and Ry went into the small establishment and bypassed the six plastic booths—three on each side of the aisle—that led straight to the clean white counter.

At the counter they gave their orders to a boy they both knew. After Ry paid him, they asked about his family and by the time he'd finished answering, a girl from behind him brought up their order.

"Uh...we're s'pose to be closin' up," the boy informed them shyly then.

"We'll just sit outside," Ry assured him.

It was hardly a comedown from the hard-seated booths inside. Tallie and Ry took their food and drinks to one of the four redwood picnic tables that surrounded a giant crab apple tree in full pink bloom beside the place.

"Guess maybe we should have brought the truck. We'd have had a more comfortable place to sit. And it looks like tonight's drive-in dessert is pretty tasty," Ry joked with a nod in the direction of the old Ford Fairlane parked under the car-service canopy. Inside the two teenagers were no longer interested in anything but each other. They were locked together in some heavy-duty kissing.

One glance at that, and Tallie's body temperature jumped about twenty degrees. She was grateful to be out in the cool night air.

"This is nice," she assured him, but her voice cracked and gave away the fact that she'd had a sudden and very vivid flash of herself and Ry doing just what those teenage lovers were doing.

She made sure to sit with her back to the carport.

"Nice enough, I guess," Ry said, only agreeing partly, as if he wasn't altogether sure that they were the luckier of the two couples.

"Did Buzz get in to see you all right today?" he asked then, as they both unwrapped their food and settled in to eat.

His grandfather had saved her a trip out to the ranch this once because he'd come into town looking to buy an anniversary gift for Ry's parents. After years of estrangement from Ry's mother because Buzz had disapproved of her marriage, the old man made sure to let her know all was forgiven by religiously honoring her anniversaries now.

"He came in a little after four this afternoon," Tallie said. "He was tired by then, though, so I don't think we did much good."

"He's doing okay, isn't he?"

"He's doing fine. He complains but he works hard," she assured, not thrilled that they'd reverted to the kind of conversation that had been the norm before the day Ry had walked in with Andrew and things between them had changed. Given her druthers, she'd have chosen an elaboration on what he'd said earlier about looking forward to seeing her tonight, not going back to the impersonal discussions of his grandfather's health and progress.

But there wasn't much she could do to alter

the program since she couldn't think of anything more intimate to talk about, either.

The tone didn't improve a moment later in spite of the fact that Ry changed the subject. "Do you think you could include some lessons about giving Andrew a bath and a hair wash when you come by tomorrow? And maybe one or two about feedin' him?"

There was nothing for Tallie to do but go with the flow, so she said, "Let me guess— your first twenty-four hours as a dad didn't go too smoothly."

"You can say that again. I never did get as much food *in* him as I got *on* him today. Took me till lunchtime to give him breakfast and wrestle with him to clean up the oatmeal he dumped on his head. Then we started all over again—for lunch he knocked a bowl of that canned spaghetti for kids off that high-chair contraption, got it all over the floor, the cupboards, the refrigerator, you name it. Without Junebug there to clean up, I had to do it. I didn't get squat done in the way of work the rest of the afternoon, and during the one trip I made to the barn after dinner tonight to look in on a mare I have about ready to foal, that boy found himself a pile of dung, mucked around in it, helped himself to a bite and seemed to like it better than anything I tried to get him to eat today."

Tallie laughed and grimaced at the same time.

"Had to haul him back inside," Ry continued, "and put us both in the shower. I thought he was tough to clean up with a washcloth, but that was nothin' compared to the shower. He screamed bloody murder. I got soap in his eyes. He got soap in mine and clipped me but good in a worse spot, more than likely wiping out any chance of my ever havin' other kids. And I still saw fertilizer behind his ear after we got out."

"That's why you missed the class," Tallie surmised through more laughter, not only at his recounting of his day but at the return of that look of complete frustration and dismay on his strikingly appealing face.

"It's a wonder I got out at all tonight except that by the time I got him into his pajamas I think he was so worn-out he was asleep before his head hit the pillow. And Buzz said he'd rather watch over Andrew himself than have me around any more tonight causin' the ruckus I'd been causin' all day as the most inept nursemaid who ever lived. Said I'd likely fall on my face lookin' in on the boy, wake 'im up and start things goin' that'd last through the whole night."

Trust Buzz not to be subtle.

"No wonder you needed to wind down," Tallie said, feeling slightly guilty for giving him a hard time about missing her class after the day and evening he'd put in. And marveling at his ability not to bite her head off for it.

"So far I don't think I'm in line for father of the year."

"You'll get the hang of it."

He didn't look convinced.

They'd both finished eating and they redeposited their wrappings in the sack the food had come out of, which Ry dropped into a nearby trash can.

As she watched him do that, Tallie knew she should get up, too, say good-night and go on the rest of the way home. By herself.

But she was none too anxious to do that.

Then, as if on cue, the lights went off inside and outside of the Dairy King, and she felt awkward sitting there.

"I'd better get home," she said as she gave a reluctant sigh she hoped sounded like weariness.

Ry threw a nod over his shoulder in the direction of her house. "Come on. I'll walk you."

"You don't have to do that."

"Didn't think I did," he informed her. "I just wanted to. Unless—"

"That would be nice," she answered in a hurry, before he could bow out.

They started off across the parking lot, passing by the Fairlane again. The teenagers were still lip locked, only they were so far down in the seat they were nearly invisible.

"Think we ought to roust them?" Tallie joked to hide her own embarrassment, and the whole lot of envy that came along with it, at the scene.

"Only if you want to risk them running us down afterward," Ry joked back in a voice that had an even huskier timbre to it all of a sudden.

From the parking lot they turned south into Tallie's neighborhood. The wide streets were lined with old brick-and-frame houses. None of them was alike since each had been built by its original owners, yet there was a sameness in the conservative lines, well-tended lawns and huge trees that had had generations to grow.

Ry let his head drop far back and sighed a deep sigh of his own, only his was the sigh of a man who had had a hard day and was finally relaxing.

"It'll get better," Tallie assured him, assuming the stress he was releasing had to do with his new job as daddy.

Apparently she'd been right, because he said, "I don't know about that. I still think that boy doesn't like me. He never cracks a smile."

Tallie did. "Have you smiled at him?"

"Come to think of it…probably not."

"Just give him a little time to get used to you and his new surroundings. Think about this from his perspective. He's suddenly lost his mother and father, been passed from one stranger to another to you—who's just another perfect stranger." Tallie glanced at Ry. "You are a perfect stranger to him, aren't you?"

"We never laid eyes on each other until yesterday morning. No reason we would have. I'm not his father by birth."

That had come out of the blue. Emphatically. As if it was important to him that she know.

"I didn't think you were," she told him, not that she hadn't wondered about it and wasn't glad to hear the truth for herself.

They'd arrived at her small single-story white frame house with its steeply pitched roof, and he went with her up the walk. Three steps took them onto a front porch that was barely large enough for the two wicker chairs she had there. Tallie opened the screen, but Ry reached over her head to hold it while she unlocked the solid oak door.

"Would you like to come in?" she heard herself ask before she'd even thought about it.

"I better get back. I've been away long enough."

She didn't know what she'd been thinking to extend the invitation or what she'd have done if he had accepted it.

And yet she was disappointed to have him turn it down.

"You're probably right," she agreed.

He didn't move to leave, though. He stayed put, one arm stretched above her to hold open her screen door, leaning his weight slightly on it.

He seemed to be looking at her as if he'd never seen her before, studying her, and while she couldn't be sure in the dim glow of her porch light, she thought there was a sparkle of mischief in his eyes.

"The trouble with walkin' home is that we don't have the truck for you to bump your head on like last night."

At first she didn't know what he was talking about. Then something about his expression told her.

"Ah, no kissable injuries, you mean," she said, playing along. She surprised herself with the note of challenge in her tone as she added, "Is that the only way you ever get good-night kisses?"

"Seemed to work pretty well last night."

"And you never had any other approach?"

"Been a long time for me. I'm not sure I remember any of 'em."

"Pity," she said with continuing amazement at herself—and him—for the sudden outrageous level of flirting they were doing.

She knew she shouldn't be indulging in it. But she was helpless beneath the warmth of those eyes of his that seemed to wrap and hold her in a velvet web.

"So how *is* your head?" he asked, leaning in even closer for a look.

Tallie tucked her chin to aid his view even though there wasn't much of anything to see. "No permanent damage. Just a little bump."

He let go of the screen door and caught it with his shoulder as both hands came to cup her face. Like the previous night. And yet not quite the same.

Tonight his touch had no teasing to it. No playfulness. Tonight it was as soft and light as a cloud. An oh-so-gentle caress of big, warm palms against her cheeks.

"Hmm. Looks like it still needs kissin'," he joked, pressing a quick buss to her crown.

But when he'd done that, he didn't take his hands away. Instead he tipped her face up to his.

For a moment he searched her eyes, and she couldn't be sure if he was looking for a sign from her that gave permission or if he was arguing with himself about whether or not to take this one step farther.

But he either made up his mind or saw her willingness because he kissed her lips then. Just as softly as he was holding her face. Just as gently. So softly, so gently it was a bare whisper of a kiss.

That was over all too soon.

He stared down into her eyes again, and she thought—hoped—that he was going to kiss her once more. Longer. Firmer. A real kiss and not just a tentative peck. And she was so eager for it that she could feel herself moving almost imperceptibly forward in anticipation.

But that's not what he did.

Instead he sighed again and took a step backward, pivoting his shoulder against the screen door's edge. And what flashed through Tallie's mind when she looked up into that ruggedly handsome face was that he'd had some sort of second thought that had stopped him.

But not without difficulty.

"'Night, Tallie," he said then. "See you tomorrow."

"Tomorrow," she repeated, sounding—and feeling—dazed.

He pushed away from the screen, and she caught it. But she didn't go inside. She was glued to the spot as her gaze followed him down the walk and she wondered what a full-blown kiss might do to her when only a mere hint of one could put her in such a daze.

It almost seemed dangerous to imagine.

Ry ignored the sidewalk and went all the way

out to the center of the street, heading back in the direction they'd come, and Tallie drank in the sight of that slight swagger that was his alone. When he reached the corner he looked back over his shoulder at her, catching her still watching him.

He waved a long arm and then disappeared around the bend.

Tallie took a deep breath and then another turn at sighing it all out, trying hard to understand what was going on between the two of them and why she was so helpless to resist it even though she knew she should. Even though she wanted to…or at least told herself she did.

But the only thing she understood with any certainty as she finally slipped into the darkness of her empty house was that that simple, fleeting, sweet kiss he'd given her still lingered faintly on her lips like no longer, deeper, more serious one ever had.

And that she never wanted the sensation to go away.

Chapter Four

Ry was out of bed at 4:00 a.m. the next morning. He figured his only chance to get any work done was to do it before Andrew got up, and the previous day the boy had slept until after eight.

So before the sun was anywhere near rising, Ry was in the barn, feeding the animals, checking on the pregnant mare, mucking out the stalls.

And thinking about Tallie and last night.

He didn't know why he'd acted the way he had with her. Teasing her. Flirting with her. Kissing her...

And, as he worked, he kept wondering what had gotten into him.

Okay, so he'd had terrible trouble not thinking about her since the day they'd first met. Terrible trouble not fantasizing about her. Terrible trouble making himself steer clear of her except out of necessity so he could keep his attraction to her under control. But suddenly nothing was under control, and he was using the necessities to see even more of her. Using them to do all he'd done the night before.

It was as if he just couldn't listen to his own voice of reason anymore. The voice that kept reminding him that she was likely to go back to her old flame just the way everybody in town expected her to. Just the way she'd apparently done many times before.

But did he let that voice of reason have any impact on him?

No. He just let it ramble on all the while he was looking for an excuse—*any* excuse—to draw out his time with her. To talk to her. To kiss her good-night...

He knew he shouldn't have done any of that, but the kiss—*kisses*—he especially shouldn't have done. He'd known it even as he was angling for them with that business about the bump on her head, with that first joking kiss.

But had knowing he shouldn't be doing it stopped him?

No.

Not the first time. Not even the second time. And the second time had been worse than the first because that kiss had been on the lips.

And what great lips they were...

Warm. Sweet. As soft as silk...

Not that it had been a spectacular kiss, though, he admitted.

The voice of reason had begun to shriek at him even as he'd leaned in for that second peck that he'd been craving the way a thirsty man craves water. It had shrieked so loudly it had kept him from doing more than hardly touching her mouth with his before dragging himself back.

But just that instant of contact had been enough to leave him knowing how good it was to have her supple lips beneath his. Enough to make him want to try for a third kiss that lingered on and on...

Except that that voice had gone on screaming at him...

She could be involved with someone else. She could love someone else. She could go back to that someone else and leave you in the dust....

So, tough as it had been—and it *had* been tough—the thought of her heart possibly belonging to another man had kept him from kissing her a third time.

The problem was, it hadn't kept him from wanting to.

The whole damned way back to his truck he'd been tempted to say to hell with what everybody in town said was sure to happen. The only thing that had seemed to matter was how churned up inside he was when he'd slipped behind the truck's steering wheel.

He'd sat a full half hour there, parked at the curb in front of the medical facility. Arguing with himself. Fighting against the idea of driving to her place right then and ringing her doorbell. Of seeing her pretty face on the other side of the screen. Of yanking that screen door open and stepping into her house so he could wrap her in arms that ached to hold her as close as he could get her, close enough to feel those small breasts of hers pressed into his chest. Fighting against the need to kiss her the way she was meant to be kissed. The way he was damned near crazy with wanting to kiss her...

More than kiss her...

Suddenly Ry realized that somewhere in remembering all that had gone on the night before, he'd stopped working to lean on his rake handle.

He yanked himself out of his reverie and stabbed at the hay with a vengeance, disgusted with himself.

Torture. That's what he was doing—torturing himself. Now and last night, because whether he was sitting in his truck on a public street or standing in the middle of his barn before daybreak, he was still wanting that woman so bad he could taste it.

What the hell was wrong with him, anyway? he asked himself. A whole town full of single women and he couldn't keep himself from sniffing after one who wasn't available.

Because there was no denying that he considered any woman with any kind of ties to another man unavailable. And even knowing that she was one of those women, he'd somehow let her get under his skin.

Boy oh boy oh boy, was she under his skin...

"As if you didn't have enough on your hands already, you jerk," he said out loud, reminding himself of Andrew and his new responsibilities as a father.

But jerk or not, Andrew or not, new responsibilities or not, the truth was he was smitten with Tallie. Big time. And nothing he did seemed to be able to distract him from that. No matter how disgusted he was with himself because of it.

So maybe what he should do, he decided, was ask some questions. Find out for himself that she was pining after the guy he'd heard she'd been pining after since she was nothing but a girl.

Maybe that would turn him off.

That's just what he'd do, he told himself. When she came over today to work with Buzz and give those lessons Ry had asked for. Somehow he'd finagle a few questions about the other guy. He'd hear that she was just biding her time until her old flame came to make up with her.

And that would be that.

These feelings he had for her would go cold. The attraction would fizzle out. He'd be free.

And what a relief that would be!

He could hardly wait.

At least he told himself that's what he could hardly wait for.

He didn't even want to think about the possibility that what he could hardly wait for was just to see Tallie again....

TALLIE TOOK AN hour for herself that afternoon. Ry had left a message suggesting that rather than go out to the ranch at four—when she was scheduled to do Buzz's therapy—she go at five, do the exercises with the elderly man, teach Ry the childproofing tricks, then have dinner with him, Buzz and Andrew. To teach Ry how to feed Andrew properly.

Okay, so it wasn't an invitation to an intimate meal alone with the handsome cowboy. But it was still enough to set up a little flutter from the pit of Tallie's stomach and cause her to look forward to the evening. Even more than she already had been.

When she left work she went home to jump into the shower—her second for the day—this time using a new gel body wash that left her smelling like apricots. She even rewashed her hair, scrunching the curls into place and letting it air dry, all the while lecturing herself yet again that this was not a date she was primping for.

Still, though, she took extra pains with her mascara and even applied a light dusting of gray eye shadow that she knew accentuated her eyes. And she was unusually careful with her blush and lip gloss before dipping into her closet for clothes no work-minded nurse-physical-therapist-midwife would have chosen for a house call.

She put on a T-shirt she'd bought and never worn before. It was midnight blue with a square neckline and three-quarter-length sleeves, and it fit every curve like a leotard. She didn't own a bra she could wear underneath it that wouldn't show every seam and strap. Which was why the T-shirt had remained, with the tags on it, in the back of her closet.

But tonight she felt just a little daring—for no reason she could figure out—and so it was the bra she left in the drawer.

She was tempted to wear an equally tight, very short skirt with the T-shirt but decided that was taking things too far. No way could she do Buzz's therapy or show Ry how to bathe Andrew if she were dressed in that. So instead she settled on a brightly colored, flowing summer skirt that left only a bare hint of her ankles showing.

She also opted for a pair of strappy sandals and even did a very quick polishing of her toe nails in a deep burgundy that matched one of the flowers in her skirt.

A final fluffing of her hair and she was ready to go.

Well, almost.

On her way past the mirrored dresser in her room, she paused, hesitated and then gave in to the urge to spritz on a bit of the perfume that went with her body wash.

"This is not a date," she told her reflection just before she headed out of the house.

But somehow neither Tallie nor her reflection was convinced.

EVEN THOUGH TALLIE had been out to the Mc-Dermot ranch well over a dozen times since her return to Elk Creek, she still never approached the place without awe.

Growing up in the small town, she'd known every square inch of it and its surrounding properties. Including the McDermot spread. In Buzz's earlier days the house had been a simple, small clapboard farmhouse. But several years ago Buzz had retired and deeded the place and all the land to his grandchildren—Ry, Shane, their sister and two younger brothers. Only Ry and Shane had taken up residence. And when they had, they'd also ventured into some experimental breeding that had produced a herd of hardy cattle that provided some of the most sought-after beef in the world.

Ry and Shane had invested a portion of the profits from that endeavor into adding to the family home so that now the original structure was merely the entrance to a huge, single-story white house with Tudor overtones in a high-pitched roof, oversize paned-glass windows and pointed eaves.

The old front porch had been refurbished and now connected to verandahs on both sides of the new portion where bedroom wings fanned out to the east and west. The wings encompassed three suites each, every suite containing a bedroom, bathroom and sitting room with its own French doors to the outside.

It was very impressive.

Almost as impressive was the inside, which mingled rich painted paneling, thick carpets and high ceilings for a combined air of Western elegance and down-home comfort in the central living room, the formal dining room behind it and the huge state-of-the-art kitchen in the rear.

Ordinarily when Tallie rang the doorbell it

was answered by Junebug—the McDermots'
all-round housekeeper, cook and caretaker. But
Junebug was under the weather with a severe
case of gout and so, except for the fact that she
came by in the mornings to get things in order
and leave meals for Ry and Buzz, she had pretty
much left Ry and Buzz on their own.

Tallie thought that was probably a good thing
because if Junebug had been there the way she
usually was, the three-hundred-pound mother
of six sons would have undoubtedly taken over
Andrew's care. As it was, Ry had no choice but
to learn to be a daddy to the small boy.

It was Buzz who let Tallie in, looking a little
worse for the wear from behind his walker. He
backed out of the way in the large tiled entry
and nodded in the direction of the east wing.

"You gotta do somethin' to turn 'im off!" the
old man said.

Tallie's first thought was of Ry. Turned on. It
was much too titillating a prospect. Then she realized the elderly man couldn't have meant what
she was thinking and said, "Turn *who* off?"

"That baby. Turn 'im off!" Buzz said, pointing in the direction he obviously wanted her
to go.

Completely confused, Tallie headed down the
hallway that led to the bedroom suites on her
right. As she went, she could hear the sound of

music. Well, not quite music. Discordant notes of noise was what it really was. Coming from what she guessed to be a harmonica.

"Help!" was her greeting from Ry when she reached the sitting room—connected to his bedroom—that they'd converted to Andrew's room.

Ry was changing the baby's diaper on the bed, and for a moment that was what Tallie thought he wanted help with. But he finished that chore a moment after she stepped into the room, lifting Andrew to stand on the floor.

And all the while the harmonica noise went on, complete with a few bumps and jags as the musician had his pants fastened and was set on his feet.

"I found that thing in his suitcase," Ry explained, referring to the harmonica as if he were filling in a paramedic on the emergency condition for which the paramedic had been summoned. "The minute he spotted it, he had to have it and he's been blowing on it all afternoon. It's driving us nuts!"

Tallie couldn't help laughing. Not only at the sight of Ry so flustered but also at the tiny boy beside him, oblivious to the stew he was causing, blowing on the harmonica and contentedly dancing a stiff-legged circular dance to his own music of sorts.

"That's so cute," Tallie said.

"Yeah, we thought so, too. At first. But he won't stop."

"Have you tried just taking it away from him?" Tallie asked reasonably.

"He pitches a fit something fierce every time."

"And who's the boss here?"

"He is," Ry answered without a moment's consideration, making Tallie laugh again.

"I could take care of this," she said then. "But if I do, what's going to happen the next time?"

"Somebody has to do *something.*"

"That somebody would be you."

"I don't know what to do," he said, his frustration making him sound on the verge of exploding.

Tallie could see where his tone might be daunting to a ranch hand, but at that moment she only thought he looked as cute as Andrew did.

Ry was dressed in cowboy boots, faded blue jeans and a chambray shirt with the sleeves rolled up to his elbows as if he were on the verge of working with those big, powerful-looking hands of his. And there he was, all six foot three inches of brawny, muscular, potent masculinity once again being done in by twenty pounds of baby dressed in a miniature variation of Ry's get-up.

But she couldn't just go on enjoying the sight.

So she said, "Take it from him firmly but gently. Let him know that's enough. Give him a distraction. And if he pitches a fit, you let him pitch a fit until he sees that it isn't going to get him what he wants. But I'm warning you—if you've been taking that harmonica away and then giving it back every time he makes a peep, this time will be the worse yet."

"He makes more than a peep."

"I'll bet," Tallie said with another laugh. Then she stood back and watched as Ry hunkered down on his heels in front of Andrew.

"Okay, boy, that's enough now," he said seriously, reaching for the offending instrument.

Andrew spun out of his reach, and Ry nearly fell on his face. He caught himself just short of it, rocking back to regain his balance as Tallie swallowed another laugh.

But he didn't lose his temper as she thought he might. Instead he took a deep breath and pulled Andrew to stand in the lee of his spread thighs.

"Come on, now," he said as if he were soothing a cantankerous stallion. "Let's put this away and I'll take you out to see the horses again."

Ry carefully pried the harmonica away from the tiny tot and then bounced up to his feet before Andrew could attempt to get it back.

The baby looked from Ry to Tallie to the harmonica he no longer had, creased his cherubic face into a dark frown, opened his mouth and let out a wail.

Ry glanced at Tallie as if doubting her advice.

"Just let him go," she coached.

Ry's handsome face contorted into a grimace as bad as if someone had just shot him, and she could tell he wasn't sure which was worse—the tantrum or the harmonica music.

Luckily Andrew's fit only lasted a few minutes. When Ry put the harmonica into a top dresser drawer and Andrew's tearless hollering didn't get him anywhere, he stopped, eyed Ry as if he were the devil incarnate, then said, "Fuff?" as if it were a peace offering.

Relief eased Ry's broad shoulders, and he finally gave a small chuckle of his own.

To Tallie he whispered, "It worked!" Then to Andrew he said, "Sure. You can see the dog, too."

"'Fuff' means he wants to see the dog?" Tallie asked, impressed that Ry could translate.

"'Fuff' seems to mean dog—he says it every time he sees J.D. out back. I'm thinkin' that's what somebody taught him a dog sounds like— woof or ruff—only when he says it it comes out 'fuff.'"

"You're getting pretty good at this."

Ry rolled his kiwi-green eyes at her. "Oh,

yeah, right. I'm an expert. That's why we've been going crazy listening to that damned—danged—mouth harp all day."

The mention of the harmonica again perked up Andrew, who apparently decided to give another try at getting his favorite toy back. He said something indistinguishable, pointed at the dresser drawer where it was hidden and said, "More."

"No more. We're goin' to see the dog and the horses, remember?" Ry was quick to remind. Then, to Tallie, he said, "I better do it and get him out of here. Maybe he'll forget about that thing."

"I'll do Buzz's therapy," Tallie said by way of agreeing.

"Come on, little man," he said to Andrew then, sweeping the baby up into his arms like an old pro.

But his gaze stayed on Tallie, seeming to see her for the first time now that this minor crisis was solved. And if the slightly raised eyebrows and the trace of a smile playing at the corners of his mouth were any indication, he liked what he saw.

Which sent a shiver of pleasure along Tallie's spine.

"I'll be waitin' when you're done," he said,

sounding as if he'd be waiting for something far more intriguing than safety instructions.

"I won't be long," Tallie answered, compounding things with the breathiness of her own voice—although that wasn't what she'd intended.

Her glance followed Ry as he carried Andrew out of the room, straying down the *V*'ed expanse of his back to the tight derriere behind the two hip pockets of his jeans.

This is not a date.... This is not a date...she silently chanted, thinking that the phrase had become her mantra.

But somehow that parting hint of intimacy made it feel as if it were a date. A date she was eager to get under way. And she had to take a moment to compose herself before she went in search of Buzz so she could get to work.

TALLIE WAS BACK with Ry half an hour later, but there wasn't anything about the next two hours that was datelike.

With Andrew in tow—and into everything along the way—Tallie and Ry made a sweep of the house so Tallie could point out what needed to be adapted for Andrew's safety. Everything from plugs in all the electrical sockets to latches on cupboard doors to locks on medicine cabinets to lowering the temperature on the water heater.

She also cautioned Ry about dangers he couldn't guard against and just needed to be vigilant about—like all the trouble the tiny tot could get into by simply pulling a chair to any variety of things Ry thought were out of reach, climbing up and getting to them.

Even the laundry room—which Ry thought would hold no appeal for Andrew—was full of hazards in the form of detergents and cleaning solutions. Andrew proved her point by trying to taste-test fabric softener while they talked.

She didn't stop at the inside of the house, though. She also pointed out the dangers of the McDermot swimming pool, the unfenced yard, and warned Ry to keep a close eye on Andrew around the many animals on the ranch so that the baby didn't inadvertently frighten or hurt one of them into a retaliation that could do real harm.

Dinner was just another lesson, although Tallie didn't have too much more luck feeding Andrew than Ry did. She explained that at this age the baby was more interested in playing and was forming his own likes and dislikes when it came to foods. And what he didn't like, he wasn't going to eat for anyone.

She talked about giving him balanced and

wholesome meals. About not bribing him with sugary treats, and about making him drink milk rather than letting him fill up on the fruit juices he preferred—although she recommended the fruit juices as treats. And maybe as an *occasional* bribe.

She showed Ry what size bites to offer, how small to cut everything—especially foods the size of the child's windpipe, like hot dogs. She explained, too, that letting Andrew feed himself some things was necessary so he could begin to learn how, even if the resulting mess was a drawback.

After dinner Tallie demonstrated the best bathing and hair-washing techniques, along with warning never to leave Andrew unattended in the tub for even a moment. By the time that was all finished, the baby was obviously weary. Once he was diapered for the night and in his pajamas, Tallie showed Ry how to brush Andrew's teeth and then followed the two of them into Andrew's room, standing back to just observe as Ry put him down for the night.

Like diapering, Ry had mastered that part of his new job. He had no trouble getting the little boy tucked in. And once he was, Andrew said something Tallie couldn't decipher and then hummed a few notes that were as unharmonious as his harmonica playing had been.

Ry seemed to get the message but also seemed reluctant to do whatever it was Andrew wanted.

The big man glanced over his shoulder at Tallie, giving her the impression he was slightly embarrassed.

But Andrew repeated the clumsy request more insistently, and finally, very softly—as if he didn't want Tallie to hear—Ry began to sing to him.

The song was an old Irving Berlin tune about counting your blessings instead of sheep if you couldn't sleep and when he'd finished the first verse a heavy-lidded Andrew said, "More, more," and got the second verse, too.

It was one of the sweetest things Tallie had ever seen, and without warning she found herself blinking back a warm rush of moisture in her eyes. She knew at that moment that no matter how inept, inexperienced or uninformed Ry was about caring for that baby, Andrew's parents had made a wise choice in Ry as their child's guardian.

The baby fell asleep by the end of the song, and Tallie worked to hide the emotions the scene had raised in her. But even with her eyes dry again, her heart had been turned to mush by the man and it refused to harden up.

He crossed the room to where she stood near the doorway, reaching behind her to turn off the light. When he had, his hand found its way to her back to guide her out of the room ahead of him.

And just that simple touch made her knees wobbly, too.

"How about a nightcap?" he whispered as they stepped into the hall. "After all you've done here tonight, I owe you at least that."

That old familiar disappointment resurfaced at the thought that debt was the only reason for the invitation, and she said rather stiffly, "You don't owe me anything."

"Then how about a nightcap because after everything you've done tonight I don't feel like I've had a chance to really be with you. And I'm findin' myself not wantin' you to go until I have."

Goodbye disappointment.

Hello little tingles of delight.

"What did you have in mind?" she asked.

"Anything that appeals to you. Served outside by yours truly."

He could serve up what appealed to her, all right. But it wasn't anything to drink.

Tallie didn't say that, though. Instead she said, "A glass of wine would be nice."

"Wait right here," he ordered, leaving her standing in the hallway near Andrew's room.

But only for the time it took him to go to the

end of the corridor, disappear into the kitchen and return with an open bottle of wine and two crystal glasses.

When he'd rejoined her, he pointed with the wine bottle toward the door to his bedroom. "Let's sit out on the side patio," he said just as Tallie's brain conjured up new, tempting images of what he might have in mind by aiming her for his bedroom.

Then he went on to explain his motives. "I'll leave the door to Andrew's room and the one to the porch open so I can hear him if he gets up. Last night he did and came calling for his mama."

"Poor baby."

"I know. It broke my heart, too."

"He must be so confused."

"He's a good boy, though. He only cried for a few minutes and then he let me put him back to bed."

A note of pride hovered in Ry's voice as he motioned to his bedroom door once more.

This time Tallie went through it, again thinking as she did that he was the right choice for Andrew's new father.

But being impressed with him as a dad faded fast as she entered his room. Being aware of him as a man once more came to the forefront.

The scent of his after-shave lingered in the

air, and the essence of him seemed to be all around her, perking up her every sense.

The room was big and well decorated with fine pieces that spoke of the quiet, confident taste of a person who knew what he wanted and didn't pussyfoot around about it.

There was an antique oak desk in one corner with a high-backed leather chair pushed into the knee hole. A carved oak dresser so large the top drawers were above Tallie's head. A matching oak cabinet that, although its doors were all closed, looked like an elaborate entertainment center.

And then there was the bed.

King-size, it seemed all too comfortable and inviting with a navy blue quilt tossed neatly over the mattress, and what appeared to be several fluffy pillows at the head.

In her imagination Tallie could see Ry sitting up against the headboard, his naked chest exposed above the quilt, waiting for someone to step out of the bathroom wrapped in nothing but a towel....

Waiting for *her* to step out of the bathroom in nothing but a towel....

"Through there."

She hadn't realized she'd stalled to stare at the bed until Ry's arm came over her shoulder to point the wine bottle at the outside entrance and urge her on.

She snapped herself out of her fantasy, feeling her face flush at being caught standing there, gawking at his bed. She felt like an idiot and suddenly had second thoughts about staying for the nightcap.

She didn't know why it was, but something about the man and everything to do with him seemed to have the most powerful effect on her. And the only hope of resisting it seemed to lie in distance. The great, great distance that should be kept between them.

Which meant she should go home. Now. Not yield to the pull and spend any more time with him tonight. Especially not when she was already feeling so vulnerable to him after watching him sing that baby to sleep.

But she just couldn't do it. She couldn't tell him she'd changed her mind and was leaving. At that moment it seemed like denying herself air not to go through that door and have a little time alone with him.

So out she went, knowing even as she did that she was giving in to whatever weakness she had for him. And that she shouldn't be.

But the least she could do, she decided once the cool evening breeze was all around her, was to sit primly in one of the fan-backed white wicker chairs that furnished the porch rather than going to the spindled railing where she'd be more accessible, even though she was inclined to do the latter.

Ry didn't stop at the other chair that formed a right angle to hers. Instead he did what she'd wanted to do—he went all the way to the edge of the verandah and perched a hip on the top rail while he poured the wine.

Even at the railing he wasn't far away and had only to reach out to offer her one of the glasses.

Tallie accepted it with murmured gratitude and sat back as he took the second for himself.

With wine in hand, he leaned his back against a tall end post, hitched his left leg up to let his booted foot ride the rail, making an elbow rest out of his upraised knee.

Tallie took a deep breath of the fragrant air, enjoying the scent of the flowers growing alongside the porch and in porcelain pots hanging here and there from the patio's rafters. "Oh, just smell that! I'm dying for a garden," she said to make conversation.

"Can't you have one?"

"No time. I keep meaning to get some pansies or something planted in the beds in front of my house but I've just been too busy."

"These are nice, all right. I like wakin' up in

the morning to the scent comin' in through the window," he agreed.

That seemed to exhaust the subject, and silence fell around them. But it was a companionable silence, and Tallie used it to watch Ry as he appeared to shed the tension of the day, relaxing right before her eyes.

The moon was high, the sky clear and full of stars and it all reflected on the whitewashed porch, lighting everything just enough so that she could make out his features.

And oh, what remarkable features they were!

Maybe if his face wasn't so lean and angular and rawboned. Maybe if his jaw wasn't been so sharp or didn't have that sexy indentation just off center. Maybe if his nose wasn't so thin and defined. Maybe if his mouth hadn't been such a mountain range of sensuality, she wouldn't have found herself sitting there drinking in the sight of him and craving a closer look. Close enough to run her fingertips along these sharp crests and deep hollows of his face—a face that seemed too wonderful to be real.

And maybe if his body wasn't a hard pillar of masculinity, hers wouldn't be yearning to be pressed against it, wrapped in his arms, every curve molded to every muscle....

But as it was, she couldn't do anything except

sip her wine and will herself to stop thinking about him like that.

Which was easier said than done. Much easier.

Then he looked over at her.

"Thanks for all this tonight," he said in that deep, rich voice that wafted to her on the cool night air and washed over her like warm water.

"I enjoyed it," she assured him.

"You like kids, don't you?"

"I do. Always have."

"So how come you don't have any of your own?"

She laughed lightly. "I've never been married. I know these days that doesn't seem like the first step for a lot of people, but it is for me."

"And how come you haven't taken that first step by now? From what I hear tell—"

"Town gossip," she guessed with another laugh, knowing what most of Elk Creek was speculating about. Apparently it had raised Ry's curiosity. "What have you heard?"

He shrugged one wide shoulder as if he only had a vague idea. "That you've had a long-term relationship with your high-school sweetheart. That it's been an on-again, off-again thing for as long as anybody can remember. That it's only a matter of time before he shows up and it's on-again."

Okay, so it was not so vague. Maybe the man could do a little pussyfooting around after all.

"The gossips are right—things with Justin and me have been on-again, off-again," she confirmed.

"And are you just waitin' for it to be on-again?"

She had the impression that he was fishing. But he wasn't the type to be merely looking for something to add to the buzz around town, and what harm would it do to tell him about her past? she asked herself. In fact it might clear up any errors the grapevine could be spreading. And along with her intense attraction to Ry, she had a deep need for him not to have the wrong image of her.

"I am definitely not just waiting for things to be on-again with Justin, no," she finally responded to Ry's question. "Although I can understand how folks are figuring that. It isn't as if it hasn't happened before, I'm sorry to admit."

"You've known this guy since you grew up here, haven't you?"

Fishing. No doubt about it—he was fishing.

"Justin's family moved to town when we were in the eighth grade. He walked into my homeroom class out of the blue, and I fell in love."

"Just like that?"

"Just like that. I was a teenager, don't forget.

I asked him to take me to the Spring Fling a few weeks later, and that was the beginning."

"You've been with him since then?" Ry asked in amazement, clearly not having heard just how long-term the relationship had been.

"I've been with him since then except if you count the off-again times. And now. I'm not with him now."

"How many off-again times were there?"

Tallie laughed. "More than I can keep track of. All through high school we broke up and got back together the way kids do—over every disagreement. Then we went to the same college and kept at it for another four years. At the end of college he asked me to move to Denver with him and marry him. I accepted. We were supposed to have the wedding six months after we got there. But six months later he wanted to move to California to try his hand at acting. I thought we could stop in Las Vegas on the way and get married there but he said he didn't want to do it like that. He wanted a big wedding. Later on. Maybe in another year or two. I said I didn't want to wait that long and either we got married right away or I wasn't going to California with him."

"But you've never been married, so I take it he went alone."

"In a blaze of glory."

"And you followed him?"

"Don't make it seem like I went running after him, because I didn't. I didn't go until he'd called half a dozen times. Apologized. Begged me to join him. Promised that if I did we'd be married there. On the beach. At sunset. Soon."

"So you went."

"So I went."

"But there was no wedding on the beach at sunset."

"Nope. Just more plans to move. To New York to work on Wall Street. Then to Hawaii to run a macadamia-nut farm. It was all a rerun of the move from Denver to California. I said I wasn't going if we weren't married. He went alone. Then he'd start to call. To tell me how much he loved me. That he was so miserable without me. Please, please, please wouldn't I come to wherever he was. He'd make me more promises. He'd woo me until I buckled and joined him, hoping each time that this would be the one when he actually made good on the promises, that we really would get married, have a family, settle down. Until I finally ended up in Alaska four months ago, still actually expecting him to set a date."

"But he didn't do it."

"He hadn't even bought me an engagement ring yet, believe it or not, after all the years of this game. I said this was it—buy me a ring, give me a firm date or else."

"Still nothing?"

"He said Alaska—it's so far away from everything and everybody. None of our friends or family would come to a wedding all the way up there. Maybe at Christmas we'd come down to Elk Creek and get married."

"But this time you didn't believe him?"

"It was more than that. But a part of it was that, yes, I knew better. I finally just threw in the towel with him and moved back here."

"Doesn't seem too different than all the other times," Ry said, sounding skeptical. And maybe as if he were suffering a little disappointment himself.

"It is different, though," she assured him.

"How so?" It sounded like a challenge.

She took it, even though she didn't understand why he seemed to want to be convinced. "I started to realize that I'd reached a point where even if he would make the commitment for real, I wasn't sure it was honestly what I wanted from him anymore. I think maybe he wore me out."

"You *think* so, but you don't know for sure?"

She shrugged. "No one knows better than I do how persuasive he can be. I've never broken up with him just as a ploy and yet he's gotten

me back time and again. But…I don't know…
things are different now. I'm different. My feelings are different. That's why I came back to
Elk Creek—to start over on my own, where
I know everybody, where I feel comfortable,
where I've wanted to be all along, where I have
roots and where I can break the pattern and
stay away from him. I just decided not to live
on hopes and empty promises anymore. Not to
let myself be disappointed again…"

She'd told Ry the whole story with a note of
levity in her voice. But that last part had come
out solemnly. Because she really was serious
about it. So serious it served as a reminder that
she shouldn't be hanging too many hopes on
the man she was with at that moment, either.

So before he could say anything else, she
said, "And now you know enough to sort out
what parts of the gossip are true and what parts
are slanted."

"Folks aren't being mean, you know. Some of
them are pulling for you to stick to your guns
because they think this guy has given you the
runaround long enough, and some of them are
pulling for a big romantic finish where he comes
into town and sweeps you off your feet to live
happily ever after."

"Have you placed a bet one way or another?"

she said, her own curiosity high enough to make her bold.

"Can't bet on somethin' I don't know anything about," he said, not giving any indication if he cared and dashing a little hope that he might.

"It's late. I'd better get going," she said suddenly, wanting to escape before too many hopes got raised.

Ry had studied her as they'd talked and for another moment he went on doing that, as if trying to read her thoughts. She doubted that he'd be able to since even she wasn't sure what was going on inside her.

Especially not when talk of Justin had reminded her to protect herself even as her attraction to Ry was at full bore, making her wish that she was stepping into his arms rather than setting her glass on the wicker table beside the chair and preparing to leave.

But even if she'd been inclined to, stepping into his arms wasn't an option, as he swung off the railing, setting both feet firmly on the porch floor.

"I'll walk you out to your car" was the only offer he made.

Side by side they went to where she was parked in the driveway in front of the house, neither of them saying much.

She'd left her purse and keys in the car but hadn't bothered to lock the doors—in Elk Creek there wasn't a need—so once she got around to the driver's side Ry opened the door for her without any problem.

Tallie stepped into the lee of it and turned to face him.

"Tomorrow night's the next class, right?" he asked as they stood with the open car door between them like a safety shield.

"Right. Think you'll make this one?" she asked with a note of teasing, trying to lift the damper that seemed to have fallen on things.

"I wouldn't miss it," he answered with more enthusiasm than seemed warranted.

"Don't forget to bring Andrew. Everybody's counting on it. They want to see him. And bring his harmonica, too. Maybe he'll play for us."

Ry chuckled and made a pained face at once. And suddenly the air around them was lightened again. "That could be askin' for trouble, you know."

"It's just too cute not to show everybody."

Ry nodded, and raised a brow at her. "Okay, but don't say I didn't warn you."

His eyes held hers, searching again for something Tallie couldn't even guess at, though she had the impression he was at war with himself for some reason.

And if that were true, she didn't know whether he'd won or lost when he reached a hand to cup the back of her head and leaned in to kiss her.

But either way, kiss her he did.

Softly, tentatively, almost hesitantly at first.

Only this time it didn't end before it got better.

Instead it went on. And on. He deepened it slightly. He parted his lips over hers, urging hers to relax, too.

It still wasn't a passionate kiss—not with her car door separating them. She didn't even reach out and touch him in return, and he held her only with that single hand behind her head. But still it was a kiss good enough to turn her blood into thick, molten lava. To clear her mind of everything and anything. To make her want him to never stop...

But he did stop.

Still too soon for her taste, he rose up, away from her, letting her go.

He said good-night and stepped back so she could get into the car, severing so completely the silken webs that had wrapped around them during that kiss that when it was over it was almost as if it had never happened at all.

Except that it had. And the imprint of his lips lingered on hers even as she finally drove away.

And it was that imprint, that sweet memory and all it kept stirred up in her that made her realize that no matter how careful they were both being, no matter how much she resisted the attraction between them, no matter how completely they parted after the fact, something was starting up between them.

Something warm.

Something wonderful.

Something with a will of its own.

Chapter Five

"What? What? What?" Ry barked into the telephone when he finally answered it on the tenth ring the next day at lunchtime.

"Sheece! Bite my head off, why don't you?"

"That you, Bax?"

"It's me. You in the middle of somethin'?" Ry's brother Bax asked.

"A mess. I just made the mistake of leaving a bowl of soup within this boy's reach when my back was turned. Now there's noodles from here to kingdom come."

The middle McDermot brother laughed unsympathetically. "Not getting the hang of this father stuff yet, huh?"

"Learnin' my lessons little by little," Ry assured with more aplomb than he felt as he wiped limp macaroni off the legs of Andrew's high chair.

"How's the boy doin'?"

"He's still sizin' me up most of the time, and

I'm not sure he likes what he sees. Seems wary of me."

"I suspect you're wary of him, too. He'll probably relax with you when you relax with him."

"Thanks for the insight, Doc," Ry said facetiously.

"Anytime. No charge. In fact, there'll be a lot more of it where that came from before too long."

"You got the job," Ry guessed.

"As of yesterday when the call came in, I'm Elk Creek's new town doctor."

"Hot damn! Congratulations! Tallie didn't tell me."

"Tallie would be the nurse who was on the committee that interviewed me."

"And Buzz's physical therapist, the local midwife and now my instructor in what to do with this baby."

"A woman of many talents."

Not all of them occupational, Ry thought, remembering the kiss they'd shared the night before.

But he didn't say that.

Instead he said, "You'll like her...workin' with her," he amended.

"Why does that sound as if I'm bein' warned off the woman herself?"

"Are you on her?"

"Very funny. You know what I mean. You have eyes for her?"

"I'm just sayin' you'll be workin' side by side and you won't be sorry because she's good at what she does."

"How's she look doin' it?" Bax made it seem as if he were suddenly interested in a purely unprofessional way and Ry knew it was just to get his goat.

Giving as good as he got—and knowing his brother had only interviewed on a conference call—Ry said, "She's just your type. About six feet tall. Probably three hundred pounds. Wears her hair in a bun. Glasses thick as pop-bottle bottoms. Big teeth. Woman can hoist a full-grown man all by herself. Wrestles bears on the weekends for fun. You two are bound to hit it off."

"Buzz said she was as cute as they come and twice as nice."

"Maybe he has the hots for her."

"He thinks you do."

"Is that so?"

"Is he wrong?"

Ry wondered if he should lie and say Buzz was imagining things. But rather than that, he opted for, "There's somebody else in the picture."

"I know there isn't somebody else in your

picture, so that must mean there's somebody else in hers."

"An old high-school sweetheart she's gone back and forth with all these years."

"Just the thing to have you shakin' in your boots."

"I'm not exactly shakin' in my boots, but the last thing I need is a repeat of Shelly."

"This other guy a friend of yours, too?"

"Haven't ever met him. He's in Alaska. Where he wants her to be, too."

"But she's in Elk Creek. With you."

"She's not *with* me. And the train comes in and out of here every day."

"So you're playin' it safe, keepin' your hands off. But not wantin' anybody else to have a go at her, either."

"Somethin' like that." He wasn't doing too well at the hands-off part....

"Buzz really likes her. I liked her on the phone. Maybe you should play your hand."

"My *hands* are plenty full right now without addin' a woman to things."

"The boy could use a mama."

"Did you call just to give me romantic advice, Dr. Lovelorn?"

"Sounds like you can use it. But no, that's not why I called. Called to tell you about the job and that I'll be comin' in in a few days. Soon as I tie up some loose ends and pack my bags."

"Good. We need a doctor around here. Tallie's runnin' her tail off doin' everything herself."

"Which cuts down on the time she has to spend with you," Bax said, offering another verbal jab.

"That's right," Ry agreed, to take the power out of the good-natured punch.

His brother laughed from the other end of the phone. "You could win this one, you know. You're not half-bad."

"Guess it's the other half we need to worry about."

"Other half's pretty good. Half not bad and half pretty good. Sounds better than some guy in Alaska."

"You'd think, wouldn't you?" But Ry didn't want to talk about this anymore, so he tried a second time to change the subject. "Shall I get a room ready?"

"No. That's part of why I called. I won't be stayin' at the ranch. Gonna take over the old doc's house. It's close to everything. Save me runnin' into town day and night."

"Buzz'll be sorry to hear that."

"I'll still be out there often enough to make a nuisance of myself."

"You're a hell of a nuisance just on the phone," Ry goaded to get in a brotherly jab of his own.

"Truth hurts, but somebody's gotta tell it to you."

"Yeah, yeah, yeah," Ry grumbled.

"See you in a few days, *Dad*."

"I'll be here."

Ry hung up the phone, spotting another glob of noodles he hadn't seen before.

"Junebug'd have both our hides if she saw what a mess we've made of her kitchen," he told Andrew, who was watching him as if the cleanup were a dinner show.

"Juice?" the baby asked then.

"Uh-uh. Milk for lunch. Tallie's orders," Ry said, handing the boy a two-handled cup with a lid on it and only a small slot to drink from.

Tallie's orders. Tallie, Tallie, Tallie...

It didn't seem as if he could say three sentences in a row without her name in at least one of them. But then, he couldn't have three thoughts in a row without her being in those, too.

Of course, thinking about her all the time was one thing. Talking about her was worse. But kissing her? That was just asking for trouble.

Especially after she'd all but said she could go back to her old relationship at the drop of a hat.

But had he paid that any heed?

Oh, no, not him.

Red lights had been flashing in his brain. Internal alarms had been sounding, and he'd still gone right ahead and kissed her.

And he knew why, too. He'd kissed her because even with all those warnings he hadn't been able to resist the urge.

"Why couldn't she be just a little less great?" he asked Andrew as he sat down to feed the baby the second bowl of soup he'd heated.

Andrew looked at him as if he were crazy.

Maybe he was.

How else could he explain knowing with every fiber of his being that he should be holding himself back where Tallie was concerned, that he should be keeping his hands off her, that he shouldn't be satisfying any of the cravings that one sight of her set off in him, and then satisfying them in spite of it all?

Or at least satisfying a small portion of one of those cravings, anyway. There were plenty more cravings for physical encounters a whole lot bigger and better that he wasn't satisfying....

"So what are we gonna do about it, boy?"

"Do," Andrew repeated.

"I'm doin' it, all right," Ry muttered to himself.

What he was doing was getting in deeper and deeper with every glimpse of that damned happy hair of hers, those damned big blue eyes and that petite body just built for a man's arms. He was getting in deeper and deeper with every sound of her voice, with every minute he lost himself in fantasies of being with her.

But no matter how hard he tried, he just couldn't help it.

"So much for the feelings turning cold by hearin' about her old flame. Or the attraction fizzling out."

And so much for being set free…

Their conversation sure as hell hadn't done any of that. It hadn't even kept him from kissing her again.

And kissing her again—more seriously this time—had only heaped another shovelful on the pile. It had made him want to go on kissing her. Longer. More passionately. It had made him want to feel her breasts pressed to his chest. To fill his hands with her soft flesh. To taste every inch of her sweetness. To find his home inside her…

Just imagining it made him break out into a sweat.

He knew he had to cool off or he was going to blow a gasket.

He set the soup bowl on the kitchen table and made a beeline for the refrigerator, opening the door and standing in the chill that flooded out of it, closing his eyes and trying to force himself under control.

You could win this one....

His brother's words repeated themselves in his mind as he stood there.

Could he win Tallie away from whatever lure her childhood sweetheart might still have? he asked himself.

But he didn't have the foggiest idea if he could or not.

And did he want to take the chance that he might not win? That once again a woman's past connections could prove stronger and he'd lose out?

No, he didn't want to take that chance.

The trouble was, he seemed to be taking it anyway.

Because no matter how much he mentally beat himself up the morning after, when he was with Tallie he couldn't stop himself from diving in.

"So what's the point of it all, then?" he asked in surrender.

Maybe it was one of the dumbest things he'd ever done, but since he couldn't keep himself away from Tallie, since he couldn't resist the attraction, he decided he might as well quit trying. And he might as well quit torturing himself after the fact.

What he could still do, though, he reasoned, was put the energy into keeping his eyes open. Into looking for signs that she might be reconnecting with her old boyfriend so maybe he could get out before it was too late if it looked as if she was going to.

It was small comfort. But it was the best he seemed to be able to offer himself. And at least this time he had the advantage of knowing there was a former connection that might be rekindled.

"I guess that puts me a little ahead of the game if I'm gonna play again."

And he was going to play again because he just couldn't *not* play again. Not when his pull to Tallie was so strong that he was just no match for it. The bottom line was that he was getting carried away by the attraction whether he liked it or not.

And he didn't like it. Didn't like being helpless against his own nature, against his own desires.

But he did like Tallie. Buzz knew it. Bax knew it. Hell, the whole town probably knew it.

He liked her too damned much for his own good—

The sound of the second bowl of soup hitting the floor made him groan, grimace and turn slowly away from the refrigerator to see that he'd made the same mistake twice and had again left the bowl within Andrew's reach.

"Uh-oh," the baby said as he craned over the side of his high chair to see the resulting mess.

It gave Ry a moment's pause as he thought about making the same mistake twice in more than just his baby-feeding, hoping to high heaven that he wasn't making the same mistake with Tallie that he'd made with Shelly.

"Do you think I just never learn?" he asked Andrew.

"Yesh," the baby answered.

That made Ry laugh as he went to the sink for the sponge.

"Maybe you're right," he admitted.

But it still didn't matter.

He was counting the hours until he could see Tallie again and he knew what would happen the minute he did—his heart would race, every sense would be on alert and honed in on only her, his mind would blank to everything else and he'd head for her like a heat-seeking missile, willing to put everything aside if only he could have some time with her.

"So hang on, kid, because it looks like we're gonna take this ride again."

He just had to hope it didn't end up with his hitting a brick wall.

The way it had with Shelly...

"SURPRISE!"

The parenting class had put together an impromptu baby shower for Ry and as he carried Andrew into the medical building's conference room that night "surprise" was his greeting.

Tallie couldn't tell who was more taken aback by it. Ry looked as if he'd unwittingly walked in on his grandmother in the shower, and Andrew seemed to search the sea of strangers for a familiar face to keep him from panicking. She felt sorry for them both.

As the only one besides Ry who Andrew knew at all, Tallie coaxed the baby into her arms to reassure him. It also helped deflect some of the crowd's attention from Ry, much to his apparent relief.

Andrew didn't know what to make of it all and—with two middle fingers in his mouth—stared suspiciously at every smiling face that took a turn at oohing and aahing over him.

Ry accepted all the compliments about Andrew being a handsome boy as if they were pebbles thrown at him and he didn't quite know how to fend them off.

Once everyone had gotten a look at Elk Creek's newest citizen, Tallie steered Ry and Andrew to the gift-opening portion of the festivities. Ry wasn't too much more comfortable with that, but Andrew got into the swing of things about then, so Ry let him have center stage. He positioned the tiny tot to stand between his spread thighs where Andrew ripped wrapping paper off package after package.

A fair number of the gifts were toys, which pleased the baby, and those that were useful items Andrew merely discarded in favor of the next present.

When everything was opened, Ry again looked embarrassed as he thanked everyone in general and then they moved on to cake and ice cream.

That still didn't take much focus off Ry or Andrew, as the other members of the class used the opportunity to ask questions about the boy and share their own stories about kids his age.

By the time Andrew had had his fill of cake—two pieces and most of Ry's—he'd gotten comfortable with everyone and, at Tallie's urging, Ry handed over the harmonica for Andrew to play.

The baby turned into a ham, and as Ry's classmates all laughed and clapped and reveled in the spectacle, Ry finally seemed to relax himself. In fact the expression on his handsome, freshly shaved face as he gazed at the tiny boy looked proud.

The topic for the class—when they finally got around to it—was toilet training. Tallie used her gift of a potty chair as a prop. She talked about how to tell when a child was ready for this particular step, and dos and don'ts in the way of techniques.

Andrew—having no idea what the contraption was for—sat in it like a king in a specially sized throne, enjoying having a seat of his own. Especially one with a nifty bowl underneath that he could wear on his head and make everyone laugh once more.

In spite of the little boy's interest, Tallie urged Ry not to begin trying to train Andrew yet, cautioning him to let Andrew settle in, feel at home with Ry and get past the trauma of losing his parents and being relocated with strangers before disrupting any more of his life.

Ry, in turn, warned the first-time parents-to-be to say goodbye to their own privacy when they had toddlers, and those couples who had already experienced parenthood put in their amens to that.

It was nearly ten when the stork decorations were dragged down, the shower detritus was cleared and the class said their good-nights, leaving Tallie, Ry and Andrew alone. By then Andrew had fallen asleep in the baby carrier Ry had brought in from his truck and Tallie was feeling slightly sorry he'd brought the baby after all—it meant Ry needed to get Andrew home and couldn't linger.

But Ry didn't seem to realize that. He lingered anyway, seeming in no hurry to go as he surveyed all the gifts piled on the floor in one corner.

"Did you do all this?" he asked Tallie with a nod toward the presents.

"I can't take the credit—or the blame," she added, unsure if he'd ended up pleased by the baby shower or not. "Through most of it you looked as if you wanted to crawl into a hole."

He smiled and flinched at the same time. "That obvious, was it?"

"I felt bad for putting you through it."

He shrugged a broad shoulder within the hunter green Western shirt he wore with his usual blue jeans and boots. "Baby showers are for women. I just wasn't too sure what to do with myself. Plus it seems kind of strange to accept congratulations under the circumstances."

"Nobody meant anything hurtful by it. To this group the coming of any baby is something to celebrate. They're all looking forward to it themselves. I don't suppose they stopped to think about what had led up to your becoming a father."

Ry nodded as if he understood and hadn't taken offense. But he also didn't seem to want to venture anywhere near the subject of what had led up to his raising Andrew and to avoid it, he said, "Guess I'd better load all this stuff into the truck."

Well, now she knew how to chase him away.

Tallie didn't say she'd help; she just gathered up all she could carry and followed him outside, wishing she hadn't even hinted at anything that would cause him to cut things short.

But after two trips the gifts were all loaded into the rear of his truck and only the baby sleeping in his car seat remained in the conference room.

"How 'bout I give you a ride home tonight?" Ry suggested then.

Since his truck was the only vehicle left in the parking lot behind the old Molner Mansion, it was obvious she'd walked again tonight. When Tallie had decided to leave her own car at the house, she'd told herself it wasn't because of any designs she might have on Ry's walking her home the way he had the night of the last class. Or offering her a ride, either. Just like she'd told herself that wearing her pink silk jumpsuit with its halter-cut top was only because it tended to get too warm in the conference room.

But faced with the opportunity of sharing even the short drive with him—and not having to walk home in the sexy little sling shoes that were killing her feet—Tallie didn't hesitate to accept.

"Thanks. I'd appreciate that."

What she hadn't thought of ahead of time—and what both excited her and made her uneasy—was that Andrew's carrier had to be strapped into the passenger's side because there were no belts in the center of the tan truck's bench seat.

Which left Tallie with no other option than to sit right beside Ry.

And all it took to make her pulse speed up and for every nerve ending to rise to the surface of her skin, was for him to slide in behind the wheel where his thick thigh was not more than an inch from hers.

Of course it didn't help matters that he brought with him the cool, clean scent of his after-shave, or the warmth of that big body, or the sense of pure power and potent masculinity in all those ranch-made muscles.

It also didn't help that within her own body there sprang to life an inordinate yearning to lean across that inch that separated them, to melt against his side, to drop her head to one straight, strong shoulder, to test the hardness of that nearby thigh with her hand....

Luckily the trip to her house only took about

five minutes. Any longer and Tallie might have been ready to swoon.

As it was, as Ry pulled into her driveway, she wished desperately that he was parking on the shoreline of make-out lake instead....

But once the truck was stopped, he didn't merely put the transmission into Park and hop out so she could, too. He turned the engine completely off.

Which left only hers running.

He also didn't hop out.

In fact he angled in her direction and stretched a long arm across the seat back to crane around and glance out the rear window at the loot now in the truck bed.

"I never knew just one boy needed so much gear," he said then, conversationally and not at all as if he were preparing to say good-night.

Or let her out.

And then Tallie did something that made things worse for her—she looked over her shoulder out the rear window, too. And her cheek inadvertently brushed his bare forearm exposed by his rolled-up sleeve.

That was when she knew she'd lost her mind because in that instant she was so aware of the warm, taut texture of his skin, of even the slight tickle of the hairs that speckled his arm, that that simple, innocent contact pebbled her nipples into tiny kernels, made her stomach muscles tighten and other muscles much lower than that suddenly hunger for things they shouldn't be hungering for....

She swallowed hard, fought not to rub her cheek against his arm like a purring kitten caressing its owner's leg and turned her head to face forward again.

"It takes plenty of stuff, all right," she agreed, barely remembering he'd made a comment about the amount of things a baby required.

Get a hold of yourself! she ordered, wondering how just being near this man could reduce her to a quivering mass of desire and leave her unable to even think straight.

But the truth was, all she really wanted to get a hold of was him....

Then she got a last-minute reprieve, and something actually occurred to her to say.

"You looked a lot like a proud papa tonight when Andrew was entertaining us all."

Ry stopped peering at the presents and glanced down at her instead. His eyes were in shadow, but still she could see him focus on her. Only on her.

He grinned sheepishly. "Oh, I don't know about that. He is a smart kid, though. He watches me—when I don't even know he's doing it— and then does what I do. I read the newspaper in the morning while we eat breakfast and I guess sometimes I lick my thumb to help turn a page. Today he got a book out and did the same thing. 'Course he licked his left thumb and then turned the page with his right hand, but still…"

They both laughed, and that laughter helped diffuse a little of what was running rampant in Tallie.

Then Ry changed the subject. "How come you didn't tell me your committee had decided to hire my brother Bax as the new town doctor?"

Tallie couldn't very well say that the last thing on her mind when she was with Ry was his brother. Or Elk Creek. Or any of the many duties her own job encompassed, because her thoughts were totally consumed by him and the overwhelming response she had to every minute detail about him.

So she chose a more professional-sounding reason.

"I didn't know when I got to the ranch yesterday if he was going to accept or not. It didn't seem right to announce something he might turn down."

"That wouldn't have happened. He wanted the job. He can't wait to get here."

"Another McDermot in Elk Creek," she mused.

"More than that before long."

"He's bringing somebody with him?"

Ry frowned slightly at that. "No, not with him. The family's ranch in Texas sold and the folks are goin' traveling. That doesn't leave much reason for our other brother and our sister, Kate, to stay there. They're both talkin' about movin' up here, too."

"Ah."

"What were you thinkin'? That Bax had a woman comin' with him?"

That sounded the remotest bit jealous and raised Tallie's eyebrows.

"I just wondered. I know from his application that he isn't married but—"

"Are you interested?"

"No!"

"What are you interested in?" he challenged.

Again she could hardly tell him the truth and say: You, even though I keep trying not to be. So she opted for, "Just in getting Elk Creek a good doctor. For everybody's sake and so I can have a little time off now and then."

He seemed to be searching for something in her eyes again. Delving deeply into them as if for confirmation that she was being honest with him.

Then he must have found something to convince him because suddenly he smiled crookedly. "And what're you gonna do with that time off when you get it?"

"Maybe plant the flower garden I've been wanting," she said when what she was thinking was, I'd like to spend it with you…with your arms around me instead of just along this seat back…. Somewhere more cozy…and private… than this truck…

He nodded with only a scant raising of that cleft chin of his, never taking his eyes off her. "I'm interested in your havin' some free time, too," he admitted in a way that left her uncertain if he was teasing or flirting. Or both.

"Is that so? What do you have in mind? More daddy lessons?"

"If that's what it takes."

"If that's what it takes for what?"

"For me to get to see you. Get to know you."

"What do you want to know?"

"Everything."

"I told you everything last night."

"Nah. You told me about one guy last night."

"There's only been one guy."

"But there's a whole lot more that makes you tick."

"Think so?"

"I know so," he said confidently. "Like I already know you're good with folks. Good at what you do even when you have to do it with an ornery old cuss like Buzz—that doesn't have anything to do with your history with men. I know that you like flowers. That you've lived in a lot of different places but that deep down you're still a hometown girl. I know you're a sucker for a baby and should have plenty of your own. I know that when you smile—and it doesn't take much to make you smile—your cheeks turn into apples and your eyes light up the world. And I'd like to know a whole lot more."

She laughed, embarrassed and pleased. "I'm surprised that you noticed. I didn't think you knew I was alive."

That surprised him. "Oh, I noticed, all right. I noticed just about everything there was to notice from the first time I saw you. Standin' on my front porch. Your medical bag held in front of you with both hands on the handle like a school-girl with her satchel. All prim and proper. All business. But with that hair curlin' every which way and those big baby-blues givin' hints that there's more to you than work. And me wantin' bad to know what more there is below the surface…"

"You could have fooled me," she said wryly. "Sometimes I've thought you could hardly stand the sight of me you ran out of the house in such a rush as soon as I got there."

"It wasn't that I couldn't stand the sight of you. It was that I liked the sight of you *too* much."

"You have a funny way of showing it—running away."

"I'm not runnin' now. In fact," he said with a glance all around them, "looks like I have you trapped but good."

"Well, don't get too cocky because one shout from me and Mr. Winthrop next door will come out in his undershorts with his shotgun at the ready."

"You gonna shout?" he challenged again with wicked delight and a gaze so penetrating it heated her like summer sunshine through a magnifying glass.

"I guess that depends on if I need rescuing. I do hate seeing Mr. Winthrop in his undershorts. It's not a pretty sight."

A slow grin eased across Ry's face.

But then he said, "You worry me, Tallie. *I* worry me. What I'm thinkin' about you. What I'm feelin'…"

"I've had more than my share of sleepless nights lately, too," she admitted quietly.

That seemed to provide yet another surprise for him. "Why's that? Nothin' to worry about over me. I don't have anybody waitin' in the wings the way you have."

"I don't have anybody waiting in the wings. And even if I did, that isn't the only thing a person should worry about."

"Ah," he muttered knowingly. "Expecting things to be one way and finding out they aren't. Being disappointed and let down by somebody you're countin' on—those are some other worries, you mean," he said, proving he'd been listening the night before.

"And not knowing much about you, either. About what makes you tick."

"I'm not a complicated guy."

"Ha!" She laughed. "For all the time I've been back in Elk Creek I haven't known what was going on with you—if anything was—and now you tell me you've noticed all kinds of things. That's not *un*complicated. You've just inherited a baby from I don't know where or who or how it came to be you who inherited him, and you aren't talking about it—in fact you're avoiding talking about it like the plague. That's not *un*complicated. You keep sending me mixed messages about what you want from me—one minute one way, the next another—that's not *un*complicated."

He had the good grace to smile in concession. "Okay, okay, so maybe I'm more complicated than I thought."

But he still didn't offer anything in the way of information to clear up any of that.

"Let's just say," he said instead, "that I'm trying to sort through my stuff the same way you're trying to sort through yours."

"And in the meantime?" she said boldly, issuing a challenge of her own.

"In the meantime there's just some things I can't seem to pass up."

"Such as?"

"Sittin' here with you like this. Lookin' at you."

Looking at her with such intensity it made her skin tingle.

"Do you mind?" he asked in a voice that was suddenly quiet and husky.

She was too mesmerized by the sight of his handsome face, by all he'd just admitted, to speak. All she could manage in answer to his question was a shake of her head. No, she didn't mind... She was in the same boat.... Regardless of how much she knew she should pass up moments like this with him, she just couldn't....

His arm came around her then from the seat back, and his hand found its way into her hair, to cup the back of her head and finger the curls as if they were satin and he craved the touch. His other hand rose to the side of her neck—all but his thumb—that pressed gently to the underside of her chin to tip it up a bit more.

She watched in awe of the way moonlight gilded the sharp planes and angles of his features as he drew nearer, once more looking into her eyes, this time as if it were a way of tying their souls together. Of uniting them.

"I don't know what's goin' on, Tallie. I just know I can't stop it. I can't even slow it down. And I sure as hell can't resist it," he confided.

It was her turn to search his eyes, but all she saw there was as much confusion as she felt. And maybe as much desire...

Then his lips met hers, and her eyes closed all on their own so she could savor the feel of that adept mouth. Warm. Only slightly moist. Tender and skilled and sweet and oh so sexy...

And that's all it took to wipe away every thought, every worry from her mind.

His lips parted, deepening the kiss just at the moment she was afraid he might end it prematurely the way he had the last two nights, and again she had a surprise in store for her. Because not only did the kiss not end just as it was beginning, but he also sent his tongue—just the tip—to tease her lips into parting, too.

And when she complied, his mouth opened even wider over hers, drawing her still farther into the kiss that was rapidly turning passionate, hungry, abandoned and all-consuming.

Tallie let herself go. She lost herself in that kiss. Somewhere along the way, her own mouth opened. She let her tongue romp freely with his. Her arms slipped around him so that she could press her palms to his back, learning that it was even harder, broader, more powerful and perfectly sculpted by muscles than she'd guessed it might be.

She was all too aware of everything about him, of the feel of his whisker-roughened face against hers. Of the heat of his hands—on her scalp, on her back now that he'd reached around her to begin a sensuous massage that she longed to have on other parts of her body.

She could feel the honed mounds of his pectorals where her breasts had somehow managed to meet them, even the steely strength of his biceps where they wrapped around her and held her willing prisoner.

That kiss made up for what the previous two had lacked. It was everything a kiss should be, could be. Everything she'd imagined it might be with this man who could do so much to her with just a glance, just his nearness, just the sound of his voice.

So much more even than Justin had ever been able to do…

But that realization scared her suddenly.

It scared her to think of all the promises that seemed to be in a kiss like that. All the hopes it raised in her. All the expectations.

Promises and hopes and expectations that, if left unmet, could leave her even more disappointed than Justin's ever had.

And that made her end the kiss herself this time.

It made her pull back—though not without a fierce battle with herself followed by a heavy feeling of regret.

"Oh, Mr. Winthrop…" she called in a joking singsong to make light of what suddenly felt more serious, her voice a bare whisper that was weak with all she wanted from this man.

Ry chuckled at her jest, looking as if he, too, were having some difficulty swimming up from the depths they'd reached with that kiss.

"Time to bring in your rescuer?" he asked.

"Maybe just time to take a breather before I even forget his name. And my own," she said with a breathless laugh.

"In other words, I better let you out of here, walk you to your door and behave myself," he joked in return although his tone was more ragged than it had been before, letting her know she wasn't the only one of them who had been rocked by that kiss.

He didn't hesitate to open the door and get out of the truck then. Maybe because if he had, he wouldn't have been able to keep from kissing her again.

Or at least that's how Tallie felt.

And he didn't touch her the whole way across the yard and up onto her porch.

But once she had her front door unlocked and she looked up at him to say good-night, he moved in to kiss her again, although only playfully.

"'Night, Tallie," he said in a bedroom tone that set off a whole new set of images…and desires…in her.

"Good night," she said, hoping he wouldn't go without asking to see her. Maybe for a real date. Just the two of them. Without any other pretenses.

But that didn't happen, either.

Instead he gave her a third quick buss and went back to his truck.

And yes, she was once more left feeling let down.

After a kiss like the one they'd shared in that truck, how could he not want to take this relationship one step farther? How could he not at least ask her out for real?

But he hadn't.

And as she watched him back out of her

driveway, she renewed her warning to herself to be careful. Not to get carried away. Not to expect anything from him. Not to get her hopes up.

But caution was cold comfort in her lonely bed when she got there.

Especially when what she really wanted was Ry McDermot.

Chapter Six

Not only had Ry not asked Tallie out on a real date after the parenting class on Thursday night, but she hadn't seen or heard from him at all on Friday.

Saturday passed making house calls to people on outlying farms and ranches, and as she headed home late that afternoon she realized that that lack of contact with Ry was not helping to get him off her mind any more than the attempts she made to distract herself from thoughts of him. In fact the man seemed to have taken up such permanent residence in her head that she should have been charging him rent.

She drove through the open countryside, past furrowed cornfields, fields lush with winter wheat ready for harvesting, and fenced fields where cattle grazed peacefully. As she did, she replayed Thursday night over and over again in her head—the way she'd been doing since he'd left her at her door.

It wasn't as if talking to him about the attraction they seemed to share for each other had helped anything. She still didn't understand what was going on. With him or with herself.

He'd shown a little jealousy—which had been flattering. He'd said outright that he wanted to get to know her better. That he'd noticed her all along, even when she'd thought he hadn't. That he liked what he saw.

So if all that was true, why hadn't he made any moves to see her again? Formally? Why hadn't he asked her to dinner? Or out for a drive after he put Andrew to bed Friday night? Why hadn't she heard from him at all in the past two days?

It just didn't make any sense to her.

And what was it that he was sorting through the same way she was sorting through the residual baggage of her last relationship? she wondered. As far as she knew, Ry hadn't been involved with anyone recently. At least not with anyone in Elk Creek. And not with anyone known by anyone she talked to. In fact, by all accounts, not one of the single women in town who'd tried to start something up with him had had any success. So what was he sorting through?

Maybe he'd been referring to Andrew.

But in rehashing the conversation, Tallie felt

sure the implication had been about a romantic relationship, not about the complications of inheriting the baby. She just couldn't figure out whom he might have been involved with. Or why he was so closemouthed about it.

Was he hiding something? Ashamed of something? Was he only playing mystery man? Or was it just another way of keeping her at arm's length?

Not that he really kept her at arm's length in any other respect. Certainly not when it came to kissing her good-night. Oh no, then he pulled her in plenty close.

Close enough to get her hopes up that when the kiss ended it wouldn't be the last she'd hear from him. Or have from him…

She just didn't know what it was he wanted.

Not that she knew what she wanted, either, she admitted. Well, what she wanted beyond his asking her for a date.

"Oh, it's all just so confusing!" she shouted out loud.

So confusing and disappointing because he said things that led her to believe he seriously wanted more than to meet up with her by happenstance now and then. But he hadn't followed through with his words.

No, he'd just left her on hold.

And even though she'd told herself that it

shouldn't matter, that she was better off if he didn't pursue her, she hadn't been able to keep from hanging some hopes on everything he'd said Thursday night.

Hopes like the one she'd had last Friday at her office that he might just show up there. Pop in to say hello. Ask if he might take her out that night.

When that hadn't happened, she'd begun to hope that maybe he'd be waiting on her door-step when she arrived home after work. That he might suggest an impromptu evening together.

When that hadn't happened, either, she'd spent all of Friday night hoping the telephone would ring. Hoping Ry would call and ask her to do something.

But no. None of those things had happened.

Instead she'd been left waiting. Wondering. Wishing.

And that was the last thing she needed. The very last. She'd had her fill of it with Justin and she didn't want yet another man in her life who would wreak havoc with her emotions that way.

"So, no more, McDermot!" she vowed. "From now on, if you want to see me, you want to get to know me, you're going to have to do it right!"

Because what did she want with a man who couldn't make up his mind about her? A man who could kiss her so soundly that her head went light and her joints turned to jelly one minute, and then forget about her the next.

Talk about disappointed expectations!

She didn't need that. Not any of it. No siree.

She'd known all along that she should keep away from him and now she was all the more certain of it.

At least she was all the more certain of it until she turned onto her own street and spotted her house in the distance.

Because that was when she saw Ry in her front yard. On his hands and knees. Just finishing planting petunias and pansies in the empty beds that lined the entire perimeter of her property.

Not far away Andrew played with a small plastic beach bucket and shovel, and neither of them noticed her until she pulled up into the driveway. And at about the same time she turned off the car engine, every contrary thought she'd had about Ry in the past two days seemed to die, too, to be replaced by an even more intense softening of her heart than he'd caused before.

Frustrating. The man was so frustrating. And confusing.

And wonderful...

"Hi," she called as she got out of her car.

Ry sat back on his haunches and grinned at her. That great, heart-stoppingly handsome face of his erupted in delight as the bright June sunshine kissed every sharp plane, and his incredible kiwi-colored eyes lit up with mischief mingled with what looked suspiciously like pleasure to see her.

He had on a dusty Stetson cowboy hat that clearly had some history to it, tight, work-faded jeans, and an equally worn chambray shirt with the sleeves rolled up to mid-bulging-biceps.

Mid-bulging-biceps that snagged her gaze and made her pulse race with the urge to squeeze them.

"Hi," he greeted in return, sweeping the Stetson off his head and wiping his brow with the back of one arm in a gesture that flattened his shirt to his hard torso and set off awakening tingles in hers at just the sight.

From Andrew's position not far away, it was Ry's removing his hat—and not Tallie's arrival—that drew the baby's attention, too.

Andrew suddenly dropped his bucket and shovel and toddled in Ry's direction, chanting, "Hut, hut, hut," until he reached Ry and was awarded the Stetson—plunked straight down on his head to fall over his eyes in what appeared to be a game the two of them had played before.

Andrew laughed and pushed the hat back with both chubby hands to free his view, leaving the brim halfway down his back.

Content with his acquisition, the boy returned to the bucket Tallie could now see was filled with dirt and surrounded by a pile of broken, wilted flowers.

"What's up?" she asked Ry then.

He grinned even wider. "I brought you flowers."

"A little more than a bouquet," she said with a slow glance around the yard.

"Seemed like a good way to say thanks for all you've done," he answered. Then, with a wicked wink, he added, "Besides, I was thinkin' that maybe if I planted your garden now, you'll be able to give me some of that free time you'll have when Bax gets to town."

He was smooth. Oh, yeah, he was definitely smooth. After two days of being left to stew in her own juices, he'd managed to make her nearly forget all about it in two minutes.

Nearly...

"I wasn't sure our spending time together was really what you wanted since you didn't make any plans for it and I didn't hear from you," she countered with a bit a challenge to her tone, left over from the pique she'd nursed since Thursday night.

"Thought maybe I'd taken up too much of your time this week and you might be sick of me," he flirted. And fished, it seemed.

"Did I say that?"

"What you didn't say was if you *did* want to see me."

Oh.

It hadn't occurred to her that she might not have actually responded to what he'd said Thursday night. But now she realized that she hadn't. At least not in so many words. Or beyond kissing him back.

A kiss *she'd* cut short...

What was he supposed to think but that maybe she wasn't as interested in getting to know him as he was in getting to know her when she hadn't told him as much? she asked herself. And here she'd been thinking badly of him.

She felt like an idiot. And she didn't know what to say. She could hardly blurt out now that she was open to everything he'd talked about two nights ago.

But so many things were going through her mind that she again missed the moment to encourage him or let him know she was agreeable to taking this relationship one step further, and he changed the subject with a nod toward the yard in general. "So what do you think?" he asked, surveying what had to have been hours of work since he'd apparently also mowed her lawn.

"I think it looks beautiful. Thank you," she answered, somewhat chagrined.

"I didn't know what kind of flowers you liked, but figured these were low maintenance."

"They're just what I would have chosen myself. Even the colors—I love the pink and purple with only a splash of red and white here and there. I wouldn't have done it any other way myself."

"Good, because I wouldn't want to have to dig it all up," he joked.

"You must have been at this all day."

"Most of it."

Luckily the weather hadn't turned scorching hot as it would as summer progressed. But still it was warm enough to leave his skin flushed slightly.

"How about a glass of iced tea?" she offered then.

"Won't turn that down. Just let me put in these few plants and hose off my hands…and Andrew's…and we'll be right in."

"I'll have it poured and waiting for you."

She went up the walk and onto the porch, opening her front door and trying to think of how she could get the belated message across that she *did* want to see more of him, get to know him, spend her free time with him. But once she'd stepped inside, she couldn't resist turning to look back through the screen, sneaking a few minutes to watch the scene in her yard.

The big-hatted baby was very intently mimicking Ry by planting the wilted flowers in the bucketful of dirt.

Ry was bent to his task much the same way. The blond streaks in his brown hair glistened as if they were drinking in the sun. His big, agile hands delved first into the soil, then scooped bedding plants out of their flat to gently lay them in the holes he'd made and pack the dirt securely around them.

Each movement flexed his forearms, and Tallie's gaze rode his broad shoulders as he worked.

He was something to behold, and she was glued there, feasting on that sight, as hungry for it as if it had been years since she'd had the opportunity rather than mere days.

"Iced tea," she muttered softly to herself in reminder of what she was supposed to be doing.

It took some willpower to move her away from that screen, though, because she could have happily gone on standing there much, much longer. But she didn't want to get caught at it, so she set herself into motion and headed for her kitchen.

She was all ready for man and boy by the time she heard the water outside turn on. She grabbed a clean dish towel and took it with her on her way to rejoin them just as Ry was rinsing off a reluctant Andrew's hands in the stream that came from the hose.

When he'd finished, she dried the baby off while Ry worked on himself and then she handed over the towel for him to use, too.

"Come inside where it's cooler," she said, picking up Andrew to carry him with her. She whispered to him as she went, "I have cookies," hoping to take his mind off the bucket of dirt he wasn't happy to be separated from and the cowboy hat that had fallen to the ground beside it.

Ry followed them into the house, down the hallway to the bright red-and-white kitchen at the rear of the cozy home. Glasses and the pitcher full of iced tea, a mug of juice for Andrew and a plate of cookies were waiting on her round pedestal table in the center of the warm, cheery room.

She pointed to one of the gingham-cushioned chairs there for Ry to take for himself and lifted the tiny tot to another.

As she served the two of them and herself, the thought suddenly sprang into her mind that maybe Ry wasn't the only one of them who could do the inviting for a date. And that if she did it, it could be the go-ahead sign she wanted to give.

"I heard that Maya and Shane got back yesterday" was how she began.

"Good thing, too. I had my hands full with a broken water pipe. Maya looked after Andrew for me, and I needed Shane's help with the pipe."

Another viable reason why Tallie hadn't seen or heard from Ry. She was feeling more and more ridiculous for her own earlier negative thoughts.

"I'll bet Maya went crazy for Andrew," she said.

"She got a kick out of him. He liked her, too."

"And you got a little break from being daddy."

Ry smiled as sheepishly as if she'd discovered a secret. "It's not like I'm lookin' to pawn him off. But yeah, it was nice to be doin' somethin' I had some idea how to do again."

"It's good for parents to get away from their kids occasionally. Good for the parent. Good for the child. Being the primary caregiver doesn't mean you can't have a life of your own or that someone else can't change a diaper or put Andrew to bed or feed him or give him a bath once in a while. In fact I think you've earned a little break that isn't necessarily more work. Do you think Maya and Shane might baby-sit tonight? You could come to dinner."

"Here? With you? Just the two of us?"

"I'm not a bad cook. We could even make it a late supper, after you've fed Andrew and put him to bed, if you'd rather."

Ry grinned once more, then took a long pull of his iced tea, studying her over his glass and maybe keeping her on the hot seat just a little since she'd apparently left him unsure how willing she was when he'd laid his feelings on the line with her.

But before he said anything, her phone rang.

Tallie didn't move to answer it, but they both stopped to listen as the machine on the countertop a few feet away played her greeting and then beeped.

"Tal, honey? It's me. Are you there? Pick up. Please?"

Justin.

Panic struck Tallie as she tried to decide whether to take the call or just let Justin go on talking through the machine.

"I love you, honey. I'm missing you something fierce. 'Specially at night—"

Hearing that, Tallie made a quick decision and lunged for the phone, grabbing the receiver off the hook to mute what Justin was saying before he could say anything more embarrassing.

With her hand over the mouthpiece, she tossed Ry what she knew was a weak, sickly smile and said apologetically, "I better take this."

"Sure," Ry answered, his tone no longer the teasing, playful, charming one he'd been using since she'd arrived home. Now he sounded curt, clipped, not happy. And he seemed to have lost all interest in his tea. All interest in anything but what she was going to do about that call.

But what could she do? She thought of hanging up on Justin, but that seemed just plain weird. It wasn't as if they were enemies or there was the kind of animosity between them that would warrant that. She just didn't seem to have a choice but to put the phone to her ear and say, "Hello, Justin," although she did it none too warmly and she kept watching Ry.

She barely heard what her former one-and-only was saying—something about being afraid she wasn't there or wouldn't talk to him even if she was. Instead she was intensely aware of the suddenly serious expression on Ry's face as his brows pulled into a frown and his hand came away from his halffull glass.

"We better get goin'," he said quietly, though Tallie couldn't be sure if he was talking to her or to Andrew as he picked the baby up while Andrew was still busy eating his cookie.

"No, it's okay," she started to say, but either Ry thought she was talking into the phone and not to him or it didn't matter. Because, with Andrew slung expertly on his hip, he waved to her with his free hand and headed down the hall.

"Ry?" she tried calling quietly after him, again covering the mouthpiece so Justin wouldn't hear.

But if Ry heard her, he didn't stop to answer.

Instead he just kept going, all the way out the front door, to his tan truck where it was parked at the curb.

Never looking back.

TALLIE WAS STILL awake at eleven-thirty that night, sitting up in bed, an open book in her lap that she couldn't seem to concentrate on because she was thinking about too many other things. Like the phone call from Justin. And Ry. Always Ry...

The phone call from Justin hadn't been much of a surprise. It had been bad timing but even though it was the first contact he'd made with her since she'd left Alaska, it had hardly been unexpected. She knew the pattern well—they argued, she left, he let some time pass, then he called.

And when he did—like today—he was very charismatic.

He'd apologized the way he always did. He'd said that he knew he was wrong to string her along. To make promises he didn't keep. That she was right to leave him. To expect more from him. She deserved better. He'd do anything she wanted if she would only go back to Alaska. He'd buy her an engagement ring this time for sure. He had one all picked out. They could set a date for their wedding.

She had to admit that there had been a different tone to things this time. More of a push from Justin rather than the ordinary placating promises. More urgency. More determination.

She knew she'd shocked him by coming all the way home to Elk Creek, getting a job here. Maybe she'd shocked him right into finally making a commitment.

But somehow this time she'd listened to it all in a removed sort of way. While thoughts of Ry had kept niggling at her. Thoughts of him walking out the door. Of how much she wished he hadn't.

"I'm not giving up," Justin had said at the end of the conversation. "I'll prove to you that I mean what I'm saying. It isn't too late for us. You know we were meant to be together. I've just screwed things up so far. But no more, Tal. I can't lose you. I won't lose you!

"It isn't too late…." Justin had repeated more forcefully as he'd ended the call.

But it sure seemed like it was when she'd hung up. Because it hadn't been anything he'd told her that was going through her mind then. Instead she'd been more worried about the call coming in front of Ry and what he must have thought about it. What he might be thinking even now.

And that told her how important Ry had become to her.

Scary thought when the man had walked out the way he had without so much as a backward glance.

But he was important to her. Important enough so that not seeing him or hearing from him in two days had whipped her into a frenzy. Important enough so that his planting flowers in her gardens for her seemed like the nicest, most thoughtful thing anyone had ever done. Important enough for her to spend the whole evening still hoping he might come back for dinner after all. And planning what she'd serve him if he did...

"Damn you, Justin," she muttered to herself, realizing that the overwhelming feeling his call had left her with was resentment for the damage it might have done with Ry.

Something really had changed....

The telephone rang right then and made her jump.

Her first thought was that it was Justin again. It would be just like him to make a second call tonight. Late. When he thought she'd be sleeping. And vulnerable. To convince her that he wasn't giving up.

Once again she considered not answering the phone. Because what if he really did mean everything this time...

But since she was Elk Creek's only medical person for the time being, she knew she couldn't just let it ring.

"Hello," she said into the bedside receiver when she picked it up.

"Tallie? I'm sorry to bother you so late."

It wasn't Justin.

It was Ry.

And everything inside her seemed to lighten up just that quick.

"That's okay. I wasn't asleep. I was reading in bed," she assured him, too pleased that it was him on the other end of the line to care about the hour.

"I have a problem here," he said then, dashing a whole new set of hopes that had sprung up in her at the sound of his voice.

"What's wrong?"

"I think this boy's sick. He's been cryin' non-stop for about three hours now. He won't go to sleep. He doesn't want anything to eat or drink. He isn't happy no matter what I do with him and he's hot to the touch."

"Where is he? I don't hear any crying."

"He's in his room. I'm callin' from the kitchen."

Okay, so maybe she had fostered just one more tiny hope that Ry was only fudging this to get her over there late at night....

"Did you take his temperature?" she asked, back to business.

"Tried. But I can't keep him still long enough to get the thermometer to register. I don't know what to do."

"Is he vomiting? Any diarrhea?"

"No, but he keeps pullin' on his ear like he'd like to yank it off."

"Let me throw on some clothes and I'll be right over."

"I hate to bother you."

"It's no bother." Even if it was only more happenstance throwing them together rather than a call from him because he wanted to see her. "Keep offering him juice or water. I won't be long."

"Thanks. I don't know what I'd do without you."

Unfortunately he did very well without her in every other respect, Tallie couldn't help thinking as she hung up the phone and got out of bed.

She was quick about getting dressed but not so quick that she didn't put some thought into what to wear. She chose her good blue jeans and a curve-hugging yellow V-neck T-shirt that she covered loosely with a white blouse because she hadn't bothered with a bra.

Her hair took only a few swipes with a brush to put it in place, and, although she told herself she shouldn't, she stole five minutes to apply a little blush and mascara to replace what she'd washed off before going to bed.

A hint of lip gloss and she was out the door, taking advantage of Elk Creek's small police force to make up those five minutes by speeding through the sleeping streets and double-timing it once she hit the country road that led to the McDermot ranch.

She'd barely turned off her engine once she'd pulled up in front of the house when the door opened and she could see Ry standing there, waiting anxiously for her.

Lights both inside and outside the house gave her a brightly illuminated view of him, and he looked as if he'd been through the wringer. He had on jeans and a plain white crew-necked T-shirt that cupped every muscle like a second skin. His hair was a bit on the wild side, as if he'd run agitated hands through it numerous times, and the starkly handsome planes of his cheekbones and jaw were stubbled with beard.

So how could she still find him so incredibly

appealing? Tallie asked herself as she grabbed her medical bag and walked up to the house.

"I've never been so glad to see anybody in my life," he greeted.

"That's what every girl wants to hear," she joked as if he'd said it without the concern and frustration in his tone.

But Ry was too alarmed to catch it.

"Is Andrew still in his room?" Tallie asked then.

Ry nodded. "I've been tryin' to keep him from wakin' the dead with that scream. Good thing the place is solid and sound doesn't carry, or we'd have Buzz and Shane and Maya all up frettin', too. I put him in his bed but I heard him at the door as soon as I shut it to come out here and let you in. I don't know why he wants me in there, though. Nothin' I do helps. Fact, the more I try the more upset he gets."

"Probably because you are."

Ry closed the door behind her and led the way to his suite of rooms on bare feet.

It was a silly thing to notice. And certainly not something that should have aroused anything in Tallie one way or another. She was a nurse, for heaven's sake. People's naked body parts were her job. And his naked body parts were only *feet*.

But for some reason they were the sexiest

feet she'd ever seen, and the sight of them bare seemed far more intimate than it should have.

But then there was a sense of intimacy all around them. It was late at night. The house was closed up. Everyone else in it was sleeping. Ry was in winding-down-for-the-day mode. And bare feet. And she didn't have on a bra....

Tallie forced her gaze upward, away from those naked feet and the rest of her wayward thoughts.

But it didn't help because her eyes locked on Ry's tight derriere, and the sight of those terrific buns only added to the awakening of things inside her that should not have been awakened.

As they neared his room, the sound of Andrew's cries distracted her. Ry eased the door to the baby's portion of the suite open carefully so as not to hurt Andrew who was nearby. The wee boy seemed as angry as he was ill when Tallie followed Ry in, no doubt for having been left alone. Too angry to be compliant when Tallie picked him up.

In spite of her cooing to him, Andrew arched his back away from her comforting hand and wailed even louder.

"Mama! Mama! Mama!"

"I ache for 'im when he does that," Ry confessed as if he really were in pain when Andrew began to chant for the woman who couldn't come to him. Who would never again be able to comfort him when he needed her.

Over Andrew's soul-wrenching wails, Tallie instructed Ry to hold and restrain him so she could get a look in the ear he was tugging at.

It wasn't easy convincing the big man to use even gentle force with the child, but once he saw that Andrew was going to fight this the whole way he finally did as she told him.

Sure enough, Andrew had a raging infection in his right ear and a less severe one in his left, along with a fever of nearly 103 degrees. His throat was clear, though, and since he didn't seem to have any other symptoms, she diagnosed a simple ear infection.

Calming the baby down so she could get him to take a dose of pain reliever and antibiotic was harder still but within half an hour of her arrival, Tallie had managed to do it all.

By then Andrew had exhausted himself and fell asleep as fast as if his plug had been pulled.

Tallie and Ry tiptoed out of the room into the hall before Ry said, "Whew! I didn't think there was ever gonna be peace and quiet around here again. You worked a miracle."

"I'm good but not that good," Tallie joked again, and this time he was calm enough to catch it.

He rewarded her with a low chuckle and

joked in return, "Can you stay all night in case he wakes up and starts again?"

Don't tempt me…

"I do need to stay for a little while. I want to make sure he doesn't have a reaction to anything since we don't know his history with medications."

A slow smile raised the corners of Ry's mouth. "Now, there's a bonus I wasn't expectin'. Can you give me a minute to clean up?" he asked with a rough rub of his whiskered jawline.

"You don't have to."

"I want to. How about you go into the kitchen and raid the fridge while I'm gone?"

"I'm not hungry. But thanks."

"Something to drink?"

"I'm fine. Besides, with the way sound doesn't carry in this place, I think I'm best sitting outside Andrew's door so if something happens I'll be able to hear him."

"You're the boss. I'll be right back."

He disappeared into his own room next door, and Tallie set her medical bag on the floor, then slid down the wall to sit beside it.

Ry was good to his word, returning in short order wearing a dove-gray mock turtleneck T-shirt instead of the plain undershirt of before. His hair was combed, his face was freshly shaved and he smelled like paradise.

"Sure you won't have a glass of wine or a beer? Or maybe some tea? Or coffee to keep you awake?"

As if she could drift off to sleep with him there stirring everything up...

"Nothing. Honest."

He got down on the floor facing her, one long leg curled Indian fashion in front of him, the other with his still-bare foot flat on the floor and his knee bent to brace his arm.

"Man. Long day," he breathed then, no longer looking frazzled but with the remnants of it in his voice.

"I never did get to tell you how much I appreciate my flowers," she said to start the conversation in the direction her curiosity was urging her to. Then she added, "You really ran out of my place in a hurry today."

"Did I?" he asked with enough of a lilt to his voice and enough of a quirky smile to let her know he knew exactly what he'd done.

"How come?" she asked point-blank.

He shrugged one broad shoulder negligently. "I didn't—don't—want to stand in the way of anything for you."

"You weren't. And aren't. You didn't have to leave."

"So how did the call go anyway?" he asked,

apparently cutting to the chase to satisfy his own curiosity.

"Uh-uh. You've gotten the last out of me until you put something in."

She hadn't intended for that to sound so suggestive.

And he hadn't missed the unintended innuendo because he grinned a wickedly delighted grin. "What'd you have in mind?" he asked with a full measure of innuendo in his own tone.

"I've blabbed all about my past with Justin, but you keep playing mystery man and not telling me anything," she said, ignoring the blush her other comment had caused and wondering if the late hour was what was making her so brave. Or maybe it was the sense of intimacy that seemed to surround them again there in that quiet hallway.

"Mystery man?" he repeated dubiously.

"What would you call it?"

He made a face that scrunched up his features and scratched his temple. "Guess I'd call it not bein' too proud of my past."

"Did you do something bad?"

"No. Just dumb."

"How so?"

But he still wasn't eager to tell her because he frowned for the second time that day and didn't rush into an explanation.

In fact he paused so long she didn't think she was going to get one at all.

"Come on," she urged. "I showed you mine." Oh, she really was brave tonight…

That made him smile slightly. "Not yet you haven't," he countered with a challenge. But then he said, "About three years ago—Shane and I'd been up here a good seven by then—I got word that my best friend growin' up in Texas had been thrown from a horse, broke his back. He was laid up long-term in the hospital, needed surgery if he was to have any chance of ever walkin' again. The ranch he'd saved his whole life for was goin' down the drain—he was in danger of losin' it. Shane and I talked it over, decided he could handle things up here alone for a while so I could go down to Texas and run Dirk's place until Dirk could do it himself again."

"That doesn't sound dumb to me. It sounds pretty generous."

"Yeah, well…I went. Dirk was in bad shape, but I think it helped to know I was willing to work his place for as long as it took. About the second week I was there, I came in from the fields one day to find a woman and a home-cooked meal waitin' for me. Shelly. Said she was a neighbor. Said folks were glad to see somebody helpin' Dirk out. She thought I could use some good food."

"She was just being neighborly."

"Mmm. The ranch was in a small town quite a ways from where we'd all grown up. I didn't know anybody and was workin' too hard to socialize so it was nice to have somebody make the effort and come to me, nice to have somebody but myself and Dirk's dog to talk to."

"And one thing led to another...." Tallie urged when he seemed to stall.

"I fell head over heels for her," he supplied flatly.

"I haven't heard anything dumb yet."

"What I didn't know was that she'd been involved with Dirk all along. That she'd been tryin' to get him to marry her and he'd been draggin' his feet about it. So behind my back she was visiting him in the hospital and then in rehab, usin' me to make him jealous."

"Ouch. Didn't Dirk say anything to you?"

"I didn't get in to see him much. The hospital was a two-hour drive away, and after his surgery they moved him to a rehabilitation center in Dallas, which was farther still. I had my hands full with his ranch, couldn't spare the time to go all the way there. We'd talk on the phone a couple of times a week and I thought he was actin' kind of strange—standoffish, businesslike, almost as if I was some sort of hired hand he could barely tolerate. But the man was fightin' to walk again, not knowin' how he'd come out of this. I figured he had a right to be distracted and preoccupied and surly. I had no idea what Shelly was doin' between us, and he didn't ever say anything. Guess as much as it irked him, he needed my help so he just kept his mouth shut."

"And you really loved her."

"Dumb. Real dumb."

"It doesn't sound like there was any way you could have known what was going on."

"Should have seen the signs. She knew her way around his house too well not to have spent a lot of time there before. There were a few comments here and there that should have clued me in. But I was blind to everything but her."

"What happened?"

"Her ploy worked. I proposed. Learned later that she used it to give Dirk an ultimatum. Said either he married her or she married me. He didn't want her marryin' me, so he popped the question. When she turned me down, she told me the whole story. Left me and Dirk both with hard feelings between us, and me with a tough lesson in steering clear of women with other entanglements."

There was a message in that. But rather than

pursue it, she worked to fit in the more important piece of the puzzle he was finally revealing to her.

"And Andrew is their son," she said, remembering that Ry had announced that the day he'd brought the baby home with him.

Ry gave a harsh, mirthless chuckle at that. "Believe it or not. I'd proposed just before Dirk was set to leave rehab and come home—walkin' again, luckily. Figured Shelly could come back here with me. Then everything blew up and I got the hell out of there. Never heard from either of them again until their lawyer called to say they'd both been killed in a car accident and they'd named me the boy's guardian."

"They never asked you if you were willing?"

"Not a word. I didn't even know they had a kid."

"And you took him anyway?" Tallie marveled.

Ry did another of those wry halfchuckles. "Thought about sayin' no, believe me. But that boy didn't have a hand in any of my hurt. And he was alone in the world. Neither Shelly nor Dirk had family. Andrew would have been chucked into the system. Maya told me his chances of bein' adopted were lower because he wasn't a newborn, which meant he could spend his whole life goin' from one foster home to another. I thought about the way things were between Dirk and me as kids and before the deal with Shelly, and I couldn't let that happen to his boy. No matter how things had ended up between us later on."

Tallie studied the man sitting only inches away from her and couldn't help thinking that no matter what kind of man Dirk had been, Shelly had lost out when she hadn't chosen Ry. He was gorgeous, personable, funny, sweet, thoughtful, charming, sexy and had the integrity to accept a job thrust upon him even by people who had done him wrong. What more could anyone ask for?

"You're a good guy, Ry McDermot."

That made him color slightly and frown yet again in embarrassment she hadn't wanted to cause.

"Good guy. Nice guy. Does that mean I'm bound to finish last?"

"Not in anything I can think of."

He smiled at her then in a way that made her heart throb—devilish and mischievous and in-sinuative. "What did you have in mind?" he said again, more emphatically.

What she had in mind at that moment—along with what a terrific person he was—was also how close together they were. How ruggedly handsome he was. How wonderful he smelled. And how naked his feet were....

And she truly couldn't fathom anyone choosing another man over this one.

She didn't answer his question, but he didn't seem to notice because suddenly the air around them fairly crackled with sexual energy that was turning things serious again. Not serious in the way they'd been moments before, talking about what had obviously wounded him deeply. What was happening between them now wasn't anything sad; it was just a renewed awareness of each other, of the fact that they were alone and that nothing—not even space—was keeping them from acting on the intense attraction that was once more firing up full blast all on its own.

"This is what *I* have in mind," he said then in a deep, quiet voice.

He leaned forward, reaching a hand to the back of her head to pull her to meet him halfway. Looking into her eyes, those bright green ones of his seemed to search for a sign that she might not want him to do this.

But there couldn't have been any such sign, because she did want him to. So much she tilted her chin a little to let him know.

His supple mouth came over hers then, softly, flirtatiously, teasing her with short kisses that ended before they began.

Until about the fourth or fifth one.

Then he kissed her for real.

His parted lips pressed to hers and stayed there, first lightly, then more firmly, more insistently.

She'd braced herself with a hand on the floor near his upraised leg, and into her mind's eye crept the image of those bare feet of his again—one of them mere inches away.

It was crazy, but her hand was drawn like a magnet to slide to his instep and then farther up, closing around his ankle as if it were a pole for her to hang on to.

She was definitely brave tonight!

Because once she got that far, she actually slid her hand up a little farther, under his jeans to the very beginning of a thick, muscular, hairy calf.

It seemed like the most brash, daring thing she'd ever done. The trouble was, when she'd done that she just wanted to do more.

His mouth was working wonders over hers, open now, urging hers to open, too. His tongue was visiting in slow, enticing motions that hypnotized hers into following suit, and while his right hand was still cradling her head, his left had come to rest on the side of her neck, inside her shirt collar—and his thumb was brushing feather-light circles there that lit sparks in her blood to glitter all through her.

And as great as it all felt, she kept thinking about that broad back, about the way it had looked as he'd bent to plant flowers today, about how it would feel beneath her palms....

He pulled her closer just then, only a bit, but it gave her the excuse to raise her hands to his shoulders. Wide, masculine shoulders. And from there it was a mere slide downward to his back....

She almost sighed out loud, it felt so good!

It was a work of art to behold and even better than that to feel. Wide, solid, strong...

But even that simple T-shirt he had on was too much of a separation for her when she craved more of him bare than his feet.

Their kisses had turned hungry by then, and as his tongue delved deeply into her mouth, learning every inch of it, toying with her tongue, teasing, dancing, fencing, Tallie gave in not only to the power of that kiss but also to her own burning desire to slip her hands up under his T-shirt, to lay her palms against the hot, hard-muscled flesh of his back.

And with that he proved she wasn't the only one wanting more, because he pulled her up onto his lap.

She felt the hard ridge of him against her hip

as he slipped his hands under her outer shirt, too, massaging her shoulder blades with a motion she longed to have somewhere else on her body.

This time it was her own T-shirt that acted as an intolerable barrier, and she wished she hadn't worn it, that there had been only one layer for him to get past, because as much as her hands had ached to feel his bare skin, her bare skin was more desperate for the touch of his hands. Her bare skin. Her bare breasts…

If her mouth had been free, she might have cried out for him to touch them. To answer her overwhelming need her spine arched in a message she couldn't keep from giving.

A message Ry was tuned in to because he finally trailed a slow path to her yearning breast, covering it with one massive, adept hand.

Her nipple kerneled into his palm at that first touch, that first gentle squeeze, and an involuntary sigh of pleasure escaped from her throat.

If only she was rid of that T-shirt!

Curve hugging or not, it was still keeping her from feeling more of what she wanted so desperately to feel. She didn't know how to convey that to Ry. She could only press her own hands more firmly to his bare back, giving a sensual massage of her own.

He got the idea. Or maybe it was just his own

idea, but he finally found his way under her T-shirt, too, found his way back to the breast he'd abandoned to get there.

Bliss! If it had felt good to have his hand on her breast from outside her shirt, it felt a hundred times better to have it on the inside. Warm and callused and tender and so, so talented, his hand kneaded her achingly alive flesh, circled the sensitive aureole, rolled the hardened crest between expert fingers that drove her nearly to a frenzy.

Feelings welled up in her that she couldn't control. Wanting him. Wanting him to make love to her—right there on the hall floor. Wanting to know every inch of his man's body.

But wanting more, too.

Feelings she'd felt a long time ago for Justin came now for Ry.

Feelings that scared her to death when she realized that nothing that was between them was as solid as his body.

And for no reason she could understand, she started to think about all Ry had told her tonight. All he'd been through. The mark it had left on him.

And now that she knew, she also knew how gun-shy he was and why.

As gun-shy as *she* was, when it came right down to it...

"We should stop," she heard herself say as she pulled away from his kiss.

It didn't take more than that for him to straighten up, to slip his hand from her straining flesh. It did take a little longer, though, for him to seem to emerge from the passion that had been swirling around them.

He closed his eyes, raised his eyebrows and nodded a silent agreement that almost looked painful.

"You're right," he said finally in a husky voice that let her know it wasn't easy for him not to go on. Not any easier than it was for her.

"It isn't that I don't want to…."

"I know. It's been a day too full of pasts and other people," he said. "This needs to come from a time that's all our own."

Tallie let her head drop to his shoulder, awash in a whole new rush of emotions for the man who, just by being kind and understanding, was making it even harder to do what she knew she needed to do.

But she knew slowing things down right then was what she needed to do.

"It's been long enough since we gave Andrew his meds. If he was going to have a reaction, he would have by now. I'm sure he'll sleep through the night and I'd better get going."

Ry didn't say anything to that. He just rubbed

her back—outside of both her shirts, not letting go of her.

But then, she wasn't making any more effort to leave, either....

"So. You never did give me an answer about that dinner I invited you to," she said, out of a sudden surging need to know she'd see him again as soon as possible.

"Sounds good," he said.

"How about tomorrow night? After Andrew's asleep? Eight-thirty?"

"I'll be there."

Oh, it felt good to be in his arms, on his lap, with her head still on his shoulder....

She forced herself to move away from him before she threw caution to the wind and begged him to take her the short distance to his bedroom. To his bed...

He got to his feet just as she did, but rather than standing upright, he bent at the waist, hands to his knees, like a runner catching his breath.

"I'm...uh...not too presentable," he said with a slight laugh.

"Me, either," she said since she could feel both nipples still at attention against the confining fabric of her T-shirt. "Why don't I go take a quick look in on Andrew?" she suggested to give them both a little breathing room to contain themselves.

The baby was sleeping like an angel, and Tallie used the moments at his bedside to take a few deep breaths before she went back into the hallway.

Ry was standing straight again when she got there, though there was still some indication that he wanted her.

She pretended not to notice, picked up her medical bag and headed toward the front of the house.

Ry followed her out to her car, opened the door for her and waited while she fastened her seat belt before he pushed the door closed between them. Then he hunkered down on his heels so that his handsome face was level with her open window.

"This isn't easy, is it?" he said, a frown pulling his features again.

"They say nothing worthwhile ever is."

"And I think this is definitely worthwhile."

He leaned in and kissed her again—a warm, openmouthed, familiar kiss—before he backed away.

"Drive safe, Tallie."

"See you tomorrow night."

"At eight-thirty. Just you and me."

A little twitter of delight went off inside her at that thought. Of all it could mean.

But she only started her engine and put the car into gear, wondering as she drove off if it made any sense at all that now, when Justin might be seriously offering what she'd wanted from him for so many years, it was Ry who was coming to dinner.

Chapter Seven

Tallie hadn't stepped more than two feet out of the church after Sunday services the next day when Kansas grabbed her arm and pulled her away from the rest of the townsfolk who stopped on the church lawn to visit as usual.

"So congratulations are in order," her childhood friend said with a beaming smile.

"Congratulations! Was the baby you and Linc are adopting born?"

Kansas laughed. "No. I meant congratulations to you."

"To me? For what?"

"Justin called and told us the good news. He asked Linc to be his best man and even offered to fly us up to Alaska for the wedding—not that we'd let him pay for us, but—"

"When did Justin do this?" Tallie interrupted Kansas, stunned by what she was hearing.

"Early this morning. Just before we left for church. I was so anxious to talk to you about it that I could hardly concentrate through the whole service."

"It isn't true," Tallie said firmly, sorry to burst her old friend's bubble.

"It isn't? Linc said he'd never heard Justin so sure about anything. That he was absolutely certain that Justin meant it this time."

"I don't know whether or not Justin is absolutely sure this time or not, but I didn't accept his proposal and he had no business calling you guys and telling you any differently."

Kansas pulled Tallie a little farther away from the crowd. "What's going on?"

Tallie told her the whole sum and substance of Justin's phone call.

When she'd finished, Kansas shook her head in amazement. "Linc said Justin seemed serious. He made it sound as if the two of you had hashed through everything, you'd accepted his proposal and were just checking your calendar to pick a date. He said this was the real deal. No more fooling around."

"Well, that's not how it is."

"And not how you even want it to be now, it seems."

That *was* how it seemed, Tallie realized. How it seemed to Kansas. How it seemed to her. Apparently she'd been right to think that even if

Justin got serious, it might not matter to her anymore.

But what if Justin actually was ready to make a commitment? she wondered.

A part of her hadn't believed it when she'd talked to him, even if there had been a different tone to their conversation. But now it occurred to her that if he'd gone as far as to ask Linc to be his best man, he might finally mean what he said. That if she wanted, they could be married. After all this time...

So how did she feel about that? she asked herself.

And she didn't have a ready answer.

The only thing she knew at that moment was that she kept wishing the day would pass quickly so the time would come for Ry to arrive at her house for their dinner that night.

"I expected to find you on cloud nine this morning" Kansas was saying.

Tallie could see that none of it made sense to her old friend. It didn't make sense to Tallie. How could it when it just plain didn't make any sense at all?

Justin appeared to finally be ready to make good on all his promises. To fulfill her hopes and dreams and expectations.

And somehow it didn't have much of an impact on her.

Instead she was spending every minute thinking about Ry. About how much she was looking forward to being with him again. About that kiss…and the rest…the night before…

Maybe she'd developed some sort of psychological malfunction. Some blip in the sanity meter that caused her to suddenly not want what she'd wanted since she was a teenager now that she might be able to have it.

But as she explored her own feelings, she came to the conclusion that it was very possible she wanted something entirely different now. Some*one* entirely different.

Someone entirely different who, for all she knew, might not want the same things she did…

"Are you just playing hard-to-get or are the rumors true?" Kansas asked then, invading Tallie's wandering thoughts.

"What rumors?"

"That you've been keeping pretty close company with Ry McDermot."

"*Keeping close company?* I've been taking care of his grandfather and teaching him what to do with Andrew. I don't think that qualifies as keeping company." Of course the dinner she had planned did. And so did that little romp on the hallway floor…

Kansas knew her too well. "Justin's cried wolf once too often, hasn't he?"

There was no reason not to be honest with her. "I don't know. I think maybe so."

"But you aren't sure?"

She didn't know anything for sure. Not when it seemed as if maybe she should give some serious thought to the possibility that Justin was laying everything she wanted right at her door. "I didn't leave Alaska just to play hard-to-get—I know *that* for sure."

"And you *are* attracted to Ry," Kansas said as if offering a clue to help with the solution of Tallie's quandary. "Which makes things more complicated than if Justin means what he's saying this time and you *weren't* attracted to someone else."

"Complicated. Confusing. Crazy..."

Kansas laughed. "Guess I won't pack my bags for Alaska. Poor Justin. He just might have played the game longer than he should have and lost you to another man."

"I wouldn't say I'm lost to another man. Ry and I are just... I don't know...enjoying a little of each other." A little kissing. A little touching...

"Uh-huh. Sure," Kansas said as if she knew the truth behind the understatement.

"Whatever you do, don't tell anybody about this stuff. Please," Tallie said, again thinking of Ry. Of all he'd confided in her the previous night and the likelihood that news like this—no matter how false—would trigger his standoff-ishness once more. And *that* was one thing she knew without a doubt she didn't want.

"You know I won't." Kansas took a good, long look at her then, as if seeing her with a fresh eye. "I've never thought of you with any-body but Justin. I've always been sure that the two of you would end up together one way or another. It just doesn't seem possible that there could be another man for you."

"Maybe there isn't," Tallie hedged.

"Or maybe there is," Kansas countered, and Tallie realized suddenly that it had become easy to picture herself with Ry even though she'd thought the same thing Kansas had—that she'd never be able to see herself with anyone but Justin.

Linc hollered for Kansas just then, and she called back that she was coming. But before she did, she gave Tallie a hug. "Things happen the way they're meant to. Maybe all those years of Justin's stalling have really only been fate keep-ing you free for someone else."

"Or maybe I've just gone completely crazy," Tallie said with a laugh of her own.

"Been there, thought that," Kansas answered with a glance in the direction of her husband.

"Sometimes, though, that can lead you to something pretty wonderful."

"Or to being locked up in the loony bin," Tallie joked.

"I don't think so," Kansas said with a laugh before she left to join Linc and his young son, Danny.

As Tallie watched the happy couple clasp hands the moment they were in reach of each other she couldn't help marveling at the fact that Justin had actually called and asked Linc to be his best man. It was beginning to sink in that he really might be serious.

But she honestly didn't know how that made her feel.

She only knew one thing, and that was that it didn't make her any less anxious to see Ry again this evening. Or the thought of what had happened between them the night before any less tantalizing. It didn't even weaken her desire to feel Ry's arms around her, his mouth over hers, his body pressed against her.

In fact she realized the oddest thing.

She almost felt removed from the whole thought of Justin and marriage and everything she'd based her entire life on to that point.

Removed from it and, at the same time, connected to the thought of anything to do with Ry...

"OH, MAN! WHAT'RE all these marks in the table-top?" Ry groaned.

He'd been repairing a dining-room chair on the back patio and when he came into the kitchen for another tool from the drawer where they were kept, he'd discovered Andrew standing on the bench seat of the U-shaped breakfast nook, which took up one full side of the room. He'd also discovered a dozen X-shaped marks etched into the oak table that stood in the center of the breakfast nook.

"Me, me, me," Andrew said proudly, pulling his hand out from behind his back to show off a Phillips head screwdriver that he promptly jabbed into the wood to demonstrate how he'd accomplished his artistry.

Ry lunged for the tool to stop him before he could do any more damage. "Yeah, you, you, you. Look what you did."

"Me, me, me," Andrew repeated as if he were getting the hang of back-and-forth conversation.

"I'm gonna have to sand down this whole table and refinish it because of this."

The baby paid him no heed, climbed down off his perch and waddled over to the open drawer in search of something else to play with.

"Oh, no, you don't," Ry said, scooping him up to hold like a saddle at his hip while he got what he'd come for, deposited the screwdriver in the drawer and closed it.

"No," Andrew said, though whether just to parrot Ry, or in response to Ry's cutting off his source of fun, Ry didn't know.

"What am I gonna do with you, anyway?" he muttered more to himself than to Andrew.

"Juice?"

The solution to everything.

Shane and Maya came into the kitchen just then. It was the first Ry had seen them for the day and it was nearly noon. Apparently the honeymoon wasn't over yet.

And that brief thought was enough to bring the image of Tallie to mind. Along with a case of healthy envy.

"Mornin'," Shane greeted.

"Only for about ten more minutes," Ry observed.

But Shane and Maya were too lost in their own happiness to do anything more than exchange secret smiles.

Shane poured them each a cup of coffee from the pot that was left over from earlier and said to Ry, "Had a late visitor last night, huh?"

"Tallie. The boy got sick and I didn't know what to do with him. Did his cryin' wake you up?"

Another secret smile passed between the couple. "We didn't hear anything but the car outside," Maya assured him. "What was wrong?"

"Ear infection. But he's back to himself today." Ry put Andrew in his high chair while he fixed the tiny tot a peanut-butter sandwich for lunch.

"Pretty long house call," Shane goaded. "Car didn't leave again till about two."

"She wanted to stay to make sure he didn't have a reaction to what she gave him." Ry didn't look up from his sandwich making when he changed the subject as nonchalantly as he could. "Have a favor to ask of you two."

"Sure," Maya said.

"Will you keep an eye on Andrew tonight for me? You wouldn't have to feed him or anything. I'll have him all taken care of and in bed. He'll probably be asleep before I leave. You can carry the baby monitor wherever you go and just listen for him."

"Where are you goin'?" Shane asked.

"Tallie invited me to dinner to give me a break from daddyin'."

Ry didn't have to see his brother to know Shane was grinning at him.

"That so? Guess Buzz was right—something *is* goin' on between the two of you."

"Yep, dinner." Ry took Andrew's lunch to him and sat on one end of the breakfast nook's bench, letting the little boy feed himself. Maya and Shane were on the opposite end, sitting as close together as two people could.

Knowing he was about to court a dose of teasing from his brother, Ry steeled himself and launched into something else he'd been thinking about all morning. "So, Maya, you've known Tallie all your life, right?"

"She and I and Kansas were in nursery school together. We were nearly inseparable all our growing-up years."

"And you know this Justin guy she's been with."

"His family moved here when we were in junior high."

"What do you think about his and Tallie's partin' of the ways?"

Maya seemed to squirm a little. "They've parted ways before."

"I know. I've heard the talk around town, and she told me herself they've gone back and forth. But do you think this time it's for good?"

"Oh, Ry, I don't know."

"In other words you're bettin' they'll get together again but you don't want to hurt my feelings by sayin' it."

"No, it isn't that. I just don't know. On the one hand, yes, the two of them have a history of breaking up and making up. But on the other hand, this is the first time Tallie has taken herself so completely away from him. The first time she's come home, settled in, taken a new job. Usually in the breakup times she stays in flux, just waiting, I guess, to go back to Justin. So maybe this time is different."

"He called her yesterday."

"Oh." That sounded fatalistic. "What did she say about that?"

"Nothin'. In fact she avoided the subject."

"Oh." More fatalistic still.

"But she hung around here with you till two this morning," Shane pointed out rather than dishing up the razzing Ry had expected. "And those weren't caretakin' sounds I heard comin' from the hallway before she left."

"Wha-aat?" Maya asked in surprise.

"Okay, so I came out to the kitchen for something to eat and heard a few things," Shane confessed.

"You didn't tell me," Maya complained.

"We were busy makin' some sounds of our own, if you'll recall." Then to Ry, Shane said, "Next time try someplace a little more private than the hallway."

"She wanted to be near the baby's room, and it wasn't like I planned on—"

"Yeah, well, from what I heard and saw—"

"Saw?" Ry repeated with a raise of his eyebrow as his brother's story got worse and worse.

"Hell, Ry, I had to take a look. First thing I thought was that old Buzz might have fallen down and was too hurt to call out. That he couldn't do anything but moan in pain."

"What did you see?" Maya asked as if they weren't talking in front of Ry.

"Kissin'. Heavy-duty kissin'. And Tallie in his lap. Nothin' either one of us hasn't caught the other doin' a time or two before."

"That is different for Tallie, though," Maya said with a raised eyebrow of her own. "She's never so much as kissed anyone but Justin before. They got together so young that he gave her her first kiss and even when they've broken up she's always been totally faithful to him. We've even joked about how she must be the only woman on the face of the earth who's never so much as kissed but one man."

Until now.

It was music to Ry's ears.

"So maybe things really are over with Justin," she added. "Obviously nothing they talked about on the phone made much difference if she was here kissing you last night."

Kissing. More than kissing, Ry thought with much too vivid a memory of everything they'd shared. And an even greater itching to share it again. Along with a few other things he could think of…

He fought to curb both the memory and all it roused in him.

"Might not mean anything if she still has ties, though," he said when he'd gotten some control of his wayward thoughts.

"Or you might be the man to break the ties," Shane suggested.

"Ties have to be broken before. Or what they really are is just stretched. They can snap back anytime."

"Didn't look like you were too worried about that on the hall floor last night," Shane put in.

"Yeah, I know," Ry answered wryly. "You know how it is—I sort of lost track of that other stuff."

Shane and Maya exchanged yet another set of secret smiles.

"Passion is a pretty powerful tie breaker," Shane offered.

"I imagine there must have been plenty of passion to keep her goin' back to that other guy all these years."

"Could have burned itself out. Or maybe she's found herself a hotter flame," Shane suggested.

Andrew slammed his plastic cup on the tray of his high chair just then and demanded, "Juice!"

As Ry opened the lid to see if the baby had finished his milk, Shane and Maya slid out of the booth as if the talk of passion had ignited some of their own.

But as they headed in the direction of their rooms, Shane paused long enough to throw Ry a glance over his shoulder. "You aren't gonna lose 'em all, you know. Shelly was a one-time thing."

"Yeah, yeah, that's what Bax said. More or less. But it's still my rear on the line."

"I don't think it's your rear you're worried about. Seems like it's an internal organ a little higher up than that. But you know, if you don't take the chance, you lose for sure."

Ry didn't say anything to that. Instead, as Maya and Shane took a few more steps toward the hall that led to their suite of rooms, he said, "So, what about the baby-sitting?"

Shane shot him a big, knowing grin.

"We'd be glad to watch Andrew," Maya said. "In fact we wouldn't mind feeding him or anything else if you want to go earlier. Or if you just want some time to yourself to get ready."

"Thanks, but I'll have everything taken care of before if you'll just listen for him to stir."

"No problem," Shane assured him. "And don't worry about what time you get home. If you're not here in the mornin', we'll just give him breakfast."

Ry knew his brother couldn't go too long without taking the jab. "Just listen for him to cry and let me worry about breakfast."

"I'm just sayin'—"

But he didn't get the opportunity to say anything else before Maya dragged him off and left Ry with the chore of fighting more of those wayward thoughts that popped into his head all on their own and left him unable *not* to take that chance on Tallie.

Whether it was wise or not.

BY A QUARTER to eight that evening Tallie had dinner well on its way to being ready to serve.

Chicken breasts stuffed with ricotta cheese and bits of prosciutto and spinach had been sautéed and were now baking in a butter sauce. Her salad of bib lettuce, black olives, tomatoes, cucumbers and artichoke hearts was ready for the olive-oil-and-lemon dressing she'd made. A casserole of grilled vegetables and parmesan cheese kept the chicken company in the oven. A loaf of crusty Italian bread was crisping. Wine was chilling, and a chocolate torte was just waiting to be cut for dessert.

That left her free to concentrate on herself.

She showered—careful not to get her hair wet because she'd shampooed it earlier so that it could air dry. Her makeup was a light dusting of blush, enough mascara so that her blue eyes were more pronounced and a lip gloss with a hint of pink color to it.

Letting her hair dry on its own left the curls springy and shiny. She combed through them with her fingers and a few swipes of a hair pick.

Then she turned to dressing, and butterflies went off in her stomach.

She loved the slinky little silk sundress she'd bought on her stop over in Cheyenne before coming home to Elk Creek. The fabric had a black background with a bright blue, green and purple flower pattern on it. The dress was short—mid-thigh—a tank style, with twelve tiny buttons from the neckline to the hem in front.

It was the perfect sundress, cut with just enough flare to hint at what was beneath it without being binding in any way. But since the straps angled inward, it was impossible to wear a bra with it.

Not that it was noticeable, the way it would have been in a knit, but the silk flowed over her bare body like cool water and made her feel as sensual as a sexy silk teddy might have.

Probably not a good way to head into an evening with a man who could make her feel that way with only a glance of his green eyes, but Tallie was as excited for their dinner as she'd been on her very first date and she just couldn't resist going into it feeling free and feminine and, yes, sexy.

So the dress remained her choice for the night even though all she could wear underneath it was a scant pair of bikini underpants and her nipples spent a lot of time at attention in response to the chilly brush of the silk. But tonight was *her* night, she decided, and she had an anything-goes feeling. She wasn't quite sure where it had come from, but it was so nice that she decided not to question it and merely enjoy herself.

She was lighting the tall taper candles on her small round dining-room table when she heard Ry's truck pull up out front.

That was all it took to make things flutter in her stomach. And maybe a little higher, too, all around her heart.

She didn't want to appear as eager as she was to see him, so she stood rooted in place until the doorbell rang. Then she had to force herself to walk at a normal pace to answer it rather than run for it the way she was inclined.

Silly, silly, silly—she knew she was being as silly as a schoolgirl. But she couldn't help it. For the first time Ry McDermot was there with no pretense, and she would have him all to herself.

And even though she hadn't admitted it before, she knew at that moment that she'd wanted this from the very first time she'd laid eyes on him.

Yet as she reached for the doorknob, a sharp stab of doubt struck her. It came with the sudden realization that there was no script for this evening. They weren't scheduled to talk about Buzz's health or how to care for Andrew. This would be only a man and a woman, alone together in candlelight and silk. And she couldn't help wondering if she knew how to do this. At least with anyone who wasn't Justin.

Jitters. That's what it was, she told herself. She just had a case of the jitters. Last-minute jitters.

"So what are you going to do about it?" she demanded of herself.

She couldn't leave Ry standing on the porch, she reasoned. She couldn't call the whole thing off. No amount of jitters was worse than the thought of that!

Which left her knowing she just had to dig up some courage.

She took a deep breath and then another, rolled her shoulders to try to shed some of the tension in them and finally opened the door. With a flourish she hadn't intended.

"Hi!" she said too cheerfully even before she took in the sight of him. It was probably a good thing, though, because once she did, her mind went blank and all she could do was stare.

Standing there, he was a tall, solid pillar of masculinity—nothing at all like the short, stocky Justin.

He was wearing coal-black jeans that hugged every taut muscle of long legs and narrow hips. They were topped off by a plain white Western shirt as crisp as a new sheet of typing paper, encasing broad shoulders and a chest she wanted to rest her palms against. The first two pearl snaps of the collar were open, showing the thick column of his neck and teasing her with a hint of wheat-colored hair peeking out from the deepest recesses of the V. The sleeves were rolled to his elbows, leaving his thick forearms and wrists exposed—those, too, tantalizing her with their pure power.

He didn't have on a hat, and his sun-streaked hair appeared freshly washed. It was combed as neatly as the short, unruly shock allowed, but she spotted a few finger marks that told her he just couldn't keep his hands completely out of it. His chiseled jaw was clean and smooth, and he smelled of that after-shave she'd come to think of as his scent alone.

And never—ever—had any man looked as terrific to her....

"Evenin'," he answered her greeting as his

eyes did a slow roll from the top of her head to her sandaled feet and back again. His mouth eased into a smile, and the look in his striking kiwi-colored eyes telegraphed his approval even before he sealed it with a second glance—as if he just had to have another helping.

"Come on in," she invited, pushing open the screen that separated them. She suddenly became overly aware of her own house, of how the small living room with its couch and single overstuffed chair compared with his huge home and much, much finer furnishings.

But Ry didn't seem to notice anything except her. Not that he would have thought less of her if he had. She knew he wasn't like that. It was merely her own insecurities bobbing to the surface. And to prove it, he didn't even glance around at the living room she motioned him into or the dining room connected to it by a wide archway, or the kitchen beyond that, which could be seen through the second archway.

Of course, this wasn't the first time he'd been there, she recalled belatedly. He'd come inside the previous day, too, after planting all those flowers outside. When Justin had called.

But Justin was the last thing she wanted to think about tonight and, somehow, slipping out of thoughts of him was as easy as it would have been to slip out of the sandals she had an inordinate urge to shuck.

"Dinner's all ready," she said because for the life of her she couldn't come up with anything else. "I figured this was late for your supper so I wouldn't keep you waiting."

She led him through the two rooms into the kitchen then.

"Smells good," he allowed along the way. Then he added, "But so do you."

She almost said she wasn't on the menu. But she didn't. She wasn't too sure that was true.

"Let me help you carry things to the table," he offered as she took the casserole dishes and the foil-wrapped bread from the oven.

"How about opening the wine while I do that?"

"Sure."

She took the bottle out of the refrigerator and handed it to him along with the corkscrew. By the time she had their meal on the dining-room table, he met her there with the bottle and two already poured glasses.

"Is Andrew better today?" she asked, seizing what seemed the likeliest option for conversation.

"Right as rain. You'd never know he was sick last night."

"That's kids for you. But he still needs to take his medicine. All of it."

"I know," Ry answered with exaggerated patience for her repetition of the instructions she'd given the night before.

They sat down to eat, and Tallie was pleased to see him not skimp on the serving sizes he took.

"Are Maya and Shane watching him tonight?" she asked.

Ry nodded as he chewed a bite of chicken that he let her know he liked. Then he said, "I didn't get out as easily as I thought I would, though. Andrew was all ready for bed but not in it yet when I went to leave and he put up a big fuss. Some of that separation anxiety you talked about in class."

Tallie laughed because she could see that it had pleased him. "Most parents take that attachment for granted, but for you it was a nice sign, wasn't it?"

He grinned sheepishly. "Guess he's gettin' used to my looks."

"And you're getting attached to him, too."

The grin turned mischievous. "To him and maybe to some other people I could mention," he said with an insinuative look at her.

Was he honestly getting attached to her or only flirting with her? She couldn't be sure.

But either way, a little thrill of delight ran through her.

It wasn't something she could go on to talk about, however, so instead she said, "How was Maya and Shane's honeymoon?"

"They said they had a good time. I think they still are from how little we've seen 'em out of their room since they got home."

That made her face flush a little, but she didn't think he could tell in the candlelight. "Now that Shane isn't going to be written up in any magazines anymore as one of the world's most eligible bachelors, does that mean you're going to pinch hit for him?" she asked, referring to the article *Prominence Magazine* had done on Shane when he was still single.

"No, ma'am. *Prominence Magazine* wanted me in on that deal when they first asked, and I said not a chance. I didn't want all that fuss even before I saw for myself how bad it got. I'm not willing to take up the mantle now."

"Oh, yeah, it must have been a terrible burden shooing off all those beautiful women," she teased.

"As a matter of fact, it was."

"You could have let them stick around."

"Could have, but didn't want to."

"Why not?"

"Didn't run into any who were my type."

"Ah. And what *is* your type?"

Okay, maybe she was doing the fishing to-night....

"Down-home country girls, I suppose," he said, giving her the once-over again. "Girls with their heads screwed on good and tight. Who know what they want and don't play games with me."

Did he think she was playing games with him? Or was he warning her not to?

Tallie wasn't sure. He certainly didn't seem put off—which he would have been if that's what he thought she was doing. In fact behind much of what he said there seemed to be an underlying message that was intended to let her know just how high his regard for her was.

So maybe it was only a warning....

It took Tallie a moment to realize that he was saying something else, and she reined in her thoughts to pay attention.

"Of all the places you've lived, where did you like best?" he was asking her after more compliments about the food as he finished eating.

"Elk Creek," she answered without having to consider it. "Other places were nice, but they just weren't home."

"Does that mean you're here to stay, then?"

Now who was fishing? "I think so. What about you?"

"Me?" he asked in surprise. "Where else would I go?"

Tallie shrugged and, since she was finished eating, too, she stood to clear the table. "You came from Texas. Maybe you want to go back there," she said as she carried their empty plates to the kitchen.

He followed her with the serving dishes. "Nope. I'm not goin' anywhere. I'm a puttin'-down-roots sort of guy, and Elk Creek is home now."

"Guess that makes you a wise choice for Andrew's guardian—that kind of stability, I mean. Not that I doubted that you were a wise choice before."

"Is that so? Why not? I'm a single guy, no experience with kids. I thought I was a pretty dumb choice."

"A lot of people don't have experience with kids until they have one of their own. There's more important things than that to choosing someone to take over a child who isn't theirs."

Ry leaned back against the counter's edge and crossed his arms over his chest. "Like what?" he demanded as she rinsed dishes and put them in the dishwasher.

"Like that stability—that's a big deal. And like not shying away from responsibilities. Like being the kind of person who would leave his own life and work behind to help a friend—those all describe you, too."

"Pretty soon you're gonna have me blushin' as bad as you were a while ago," he joked.

Tallie shrugged again and ignored the reference to the flush she'd thought he hadn't seen earlier. "You're a good man—that shouldn't embarrass you."

"Only embarrasses me to talk about it."

She let him off the hook. "Maybe we should just have dessert, then."

His twin-peaked mouth tipped up devilishly at one corner, along with a single lascivious eyebrow. "What'd you have in mind?"

"Chocolate torte," she said with yet another laugh at his teasing innuendo.

"Hmm..." He seemed to consider it. Then he said, "Maybe later."

"How about another glass of wine in the living room, then? Or coffee? Or tea?"

"How 'bout just you and me in the living room?"

"Okay," she agreed, pretending not to notice how alluring he'd made that sound.

She led the way through the dining room into the living room, sitting on the couch—not quite in the center, not quite hugging one end. He could have sat at the end farthest from her. Or he could have chosen the single chair. But he didn't. He opted for sitting right beside her, angling slightly in her direction as if he was intent on studying her.

It was nice. And maybe a little unnerving, too, as his nearness set those flutters alight in her stomach again.

But for the most part the evening had turned relaxed, and so Tallie finally slipped her feet out of her sandals the way she'd been wanting to, slid low enough on the sofa to rest her head on the back and even propped her feet on the coffee table, hoping the casual posture would calm the flutterings.

"I saw Junebug yesterday," she said then to take her mind off the butterflies in her stomach.

"Did you?"

"She's better. She says she's going back to work at your place next week. I don't think she can wait to get her hands on Andrew. Watching him for you while you work the ranch obviously won't be a bother to her."

"Mmm," he agreed absently, as if he were only half listening while he thought about something else as he went on watching her.

"This is really nice," he said then, stretching an arm across the top of the couch and fiddling with her hair. "Thanks. For inviting me. For dinner. For everything."

"It's been nice for me, too."

"Has it?" he asked, but there was something in his voice that questioned more than that. Maybe something that was searching for assurance that what was happening between them meant as much to her as it did to him.

But she didn't know how to convey it any way but to turn her head more toward his hand where it still toyed with her hair.

"I'd like for this to be just the beginning for us, Tallie," he said then, quietly, solemnly.

"I'd like that, too," she answered, wishing for more eloquence. But with her heart dancing the happy jig his words set off in it she couldn't quite summon anything too expansive.

Apparently it didn't matter because Ry smiled down at her, his handsome face alight with a pleased expression as he drew nearer and kissed her.

It was funny how fast his kisses had become familiar to her. Not boringly so, by any means, but familiar enough to let her welcome them, to know just how to respond to them. Besides, no kiss that adept, that sweet, that titillating and arousing, could have ever been boring. No, the familiarity just allowed them to melt into the kiss almost instantly. To let mouths open, to meet and match each teasing of the other's tongue, to seamlessly pick up where they'd left off the night before as if no time at all had passed.

He raised his other hand to the side of her face, caressing it as if it were satin, urging her head back a little farther so he could deepen their kiss.

His tongue was more aggressive tonight, but only pleasantly so, leading hers in the dance they shared, meeting, circling, parting to meet again.

She sank into the soft, loose cushions of the couch, reaching a hand of her own to the nape of his neck, testing the coarseness of his hair where it was cut short there. Somehow her other hand had found its way to his leg, just above his knee, but it didn't seem out of place and she was reveling in the knowledge that his thigh was as thick, as tightly muscled as it looked.

Their kisses grew hungrier, more engrossing, and the hand at her cheek began to slide. To her neck, where his thumb traced the hollow of her throat, pausing to rub feathery strokes and teach her just how sensitive a spot it could be.

That thumb followed her collarbone from there, dragging the strap of her dress with it as far as the fabric would allow.

Things were coming alive inside Tallie. Quickly. Her nipples were pebbled beneath the silk of her dress, and it occurred to her that it was a good thing she hadn't worn a bra because they were straining so urgently against even that light material they felt as if they would have ripped completely through the containment of sheer lace. And lower still, between her legs, a warm awakening was taking place that caused her hips to clench and rise just a bit from the seat.

She tried to control it. She didn't want to squirm. But those kisses, that tender caress of fingertips so masterful, were making it difficult not to.

His mouth was wide open over hers now, wider even than before, and his tongue was more insistent, thrusting and parrying as if in preview of better things yet to be.

His hand began to move again, following the neckline of her dress to the buttons that held it closed, trailing that line of tiny fasteners to her breast.

And how silk could suddenly feel like armor, Tallie didn't know. But it did. Armor that kept that wonderful hand from discovering her bare breast and the kerneled nipple that was crying out for his touch.

Even her attempts to keep from squirming beneath him couldn't stop her spine from arching or her own hand from inching slightly higher on his thigh. A thigh he lifted over her and wrapped somewhat around her just then to pull her body up closer to his.

She let that hand on his thigh climb the outer side of his leg, over his hip to his back, to pull his shirttails free of his jeans and dive inside herself—not only to relay the message that skin against skin was what she wanted, but also to gain some of that skin for herself.

His broad back was like smooth satin over steel, and it felt so good she let her other hand join the first so that both palms could be pressed to that remarkable expanse.

But he distracted her from that when he finally sought out her buttons again, this time to undo them. One by one. With measured effort that prolonged her anticipation and elevated her yearning to new heights.

And then, when the buttons halfway to her waist were laid open, he slipped that massive hand inside and found the engorged orb that was nearly ready to burst with desire.

Squirm she did then. Just a little. How could she help but writhe in response to something that felt that incredible? His touch was much like he was—steady, sure, firm, tender. And oh, so talented…

One moment his callused palm whispered across her skin, barely skimming the taut crest. The next moment he engulfed the entire globe with a grip that was gentle but firm enough to pluck ripe fruit from the vine, only to abandon the round firmness the moment after that so he could roll her nipple between adept fingers, tracing the sentient aureole around and around until she couldn't contain the groan of pleasure that rumbled from her throat.

That was when his lips deserted hers to kiss a path down her chin, down the side of her neck, lower and lower until he captured the breast he held primed, covering it with the warm velvet of that mouth and the magic wonders of a tongue that tormented her nipple even more blissfully than his fingers had.

Wild things erupted inside Tallie. Needs too great to contain. Hungers so intense they consumed any inhibitions she had.

She let her own hands glide from his back to his front, filling them with honed pectorals and flat male nipples that tightened to her ministrations.

But there was more she wanted to know of him. Of his magnificent body. The body she craved to have naked against her own. So rather than stay too long at the chest that heavy work had sculpted, she slid her hands up to his shoulders and spread her arms wide enough to pop the snaps down the front of his shirt all in one motion.

It made him chuckle lightly and flick his tongue against her nipple teasingly, but he didn't protest. In fact he aided her cause by taking both arms away from her so she could free him of the garment.

And that's just what she did.

For a while she reveled in the unfettered freedom of his bare torso, exploring it, learning every bulging muscle, every taut tendon, letting her palms glide over each inch, savoring it along the way. And all the while she moved downward, forward, until she located the snap on the waistband of his jeans....

She fiddled with it a bit, wondering if she should pop it, too. If he wanted her to.

But she didn't have to wonder long before he reached a hand to cover hers, to guide her fingertips up and over the top edge to where the very tip of the long, hard proof of his desire for her was nearly ready to pop the snap all on its own.

Still with his hand shadowing hers he pulled open the snap himself and left the zipper partly spread, as well.

And then, in case she wasn't convinced yet, he took his hand away from hers and let it rest on the smooth inside of her thigh to slide higher and higher until he reached that junction between her own legs.

"Oh…"

She hadn't intended to say anything but his touch felt so tremendous the word—the groan—escaped before she realized it.

He didn't torture her with any hesitation, but eased his hand underneath her bikinis and went right for that spot that was already achingly in need of his attention. Of him.

He rose up from her breast to gently nibble her ear lobe and whispered, "I want to make love to you."

And in that instant she knew that having him all to herself for an evening was not the only thing she'd wanted since she'd first laid eyes on him.

She'd spent so much of the day thinking about Ry, about what had happened between them on the hall floor the night before and regretting that she'd stopped him. Wishing she hadn't. She didn't want more of those regrets. She wanted him. She wanted all of him….

"I want you to…"

He didn't need more encouragement than that.

His mouth came over hers again, wide open, commanding, urgent. The hand between her legs worked more wonders than she knew existed, slipping a finger inside, drawing it out, learning just how ready she was.

Then that hand trailed down her thigh again, taking her panties with it until both disappeared for a moment before his hand returned to the remaining buttons of her dress.

He made quick work of them, quick work of slipping the dress off her shoulders and dropping it to the floor. Quick work of shedding what remained of his own clothes and then tossing the loose sofa pillows off the back of the couch to allow them more room.

And then she was lying beneath him with the full length, the full weight of him above her. One knee eased hers apart as his mouth took hers captive once again in a profound, absorbing kiss at the same time that his long, thick shaft searched for that recess in her body that wanted him so much she thought she might die if he didn't find it right that moment.

But when he did, it was worth the wait.

He found his home inside her, fully, deeply, filling her so perfectly that her hips were drawn to rise into his like a magnet finding its mate. She closed around him as if an integral part of her being had just been returned to her, completing her.

Then he began to move. Slowly at first, carefully, drawing out, easing back in again only to draw out once more. The rhythm was just right, increasing in speed, in intensity, until each thrust was so flawless they moved together as one, faster and faster, harder and harder....

He swept her up in a vortex of divine pleasure, a swirling tornado all around her, inside her until she exploded through the spiral to a summit better than anything she'd ever experienced before. It absorbed her, encompassed her, shot her through time and space in a white-hot passion she never wanted to escape.

She clung to Ry and he to her as he reached his own climax, plunging so far into her she thought they might never be able to part. His rock-hard body was stiff and taut as he drove them past any limits to a culmination that left them both spent, exhausted and oh, so satiated....

For a time they just lay there, holding each other, catching their breath. The weight of Ry was a wonderful burden, like a heavy quilt on a frigid winter's night.

Then he rose up enough to kiss her brow, her nose, her chin.

"I got a little carried away. Are you okay?" he asked in a ragged voice.

"If I said no, would that mean you wouldn't do it again?" she joked in a tone almost as husky.

He laughed. "No, I'd just try to hold back a little next time."

"I don't think I've ever been quite so okay,"

she finally answered his question. "Don't hold anything back."

He kissed her again then, his mouth over hers, hot and soft and succulent, sealing what they'd just shared even as he pulsed one last time inside her before he pulled out.

He rolled them both to their sides so that they were snuggled together into the L of the sofa as comfortably as if it were a cocoon, settling so that Tallie's head was pillowed by his shoulder. Then he rested his head atop hers and sighed sleepily.

"Want chocolate torte now?" she teased.

"I think it'll make a good breakfast."

"Does that mean you'll be here to eat it, then?"

"I'll be here to serve it to you." He pressed warm lips to her hair, sighed even more heavily and whispered, "After all, this was just the beginning, remember?"

"Mmm."

"Besides, I believe I just agreed to a second round after you let me rest up a little."

She only had the energy to smile against his warm skin as she closed her eyes and let herself drift toward the sleep that was beckoning as irresistibly to her as she knew it was to him.

But as she gave in to it, she thought that never

in her life had she felt so replete, so cared for, so safe.

Because not for a single minute did she doubt the man in whose arms she was cradled.

Chapter Eight

Ry woke up before Tallie did the next morning. They were in her double bed, where they'd moved from the couch to share the second occasion of lovemaking in the middle of the night. An even longer, slower—and if it were possible—more eager occasion for lovemaking than the first time. Then they'd fallen asleep again, wrapped in each other's arms, legs entwined, her head on his chest.

But that wasn't how they were when his eyes opened at nearly 8:00 a.m. Tallie was still lying on her side, facing him, but she'd moved far enough away to curl into a ball as she slept.

His arm remained under her head, though, and he left it there as he rolled to his side so he could watch her.

She really was beautiful to him. Her hair was spread out against the pillow, thick eyelashes dusted healthy pink cheeks, her pale lips were parted slightly and she breathed so softly he couldn't hear it but could see the cream-colored sheet rise and fall with her body.

And what a great little body it was....

He wanted her again as much as he'd wanted her the first time. And the second. But even as desire stirred within him, there were other thoughts on his mind, too. Thoughts about how perfect it felt to wake up with her beside him. About how much more perfect it would be if Andrew were in the next room. If, after another session—or two—of lovemaking, he could bring the baby into bed with them to play awhile before they all shared breakfast. Like a family...

That thought shocked him some.

Was he actually thinking of the three of them as a family?

But when he seriously explored the images in his head, he knew that that was just what he was thinking.

Fast trip from lonely bachelor to family man, a little voice in the back of his mind pointed out. And he couldn't deny it.

He'd closed a door in his life, in his heart, after Shelly. Because of Shelly. A door he might never have opened on his own. But Shelly's son had stormed that door, and fast on his heels, in had come Tallie, too. When he'd least expected it. When he hadn't even been looking.

But the fact was, fast or not, being with Tallie

felt right to him. It felt right to be in bed with her. Right to picture him and Tallie and Andrew together in the future. It filled him with an emotion he hadn't experienced in a long time. And never as strongly, as overwhelmingly, as powerfully, as he did at that moment.

Love. Damn if he wasn't in love. With them both.

Andrew had just somehow inched his way under Ry's skin little by little, but with Tallie it almost seemed as if the seeds of what he felt for her must have been planted from the very first minute he'd set eyes on her. Why else had he been so leery of having anything to do with her? If he hadn't cared, her past wouldn't have been such a big deal to him.

If he hadn't cared, he would have been able to have some peace from thinking about her.

If he hadn't cared, it wouldn't have been so almighty tough to keep away from her.

If he hadn't cared, she wouldn't have been able to slip through that newly opened door to his life and to his heart so easily.

But maybe now it had all worked out...

Tallie sighed just then and rubbed her head against his arm. Sensuously, even if she was still asleep. And that desire that was roiling around in Ry suddenly got a whole lot more insistent.

But he decided that before he did anything

about it, he should get up and call home, make sure Maya and Shane knew he wasn't there and would look after Andrew for him a while longer.

He leaned over and gave Tallie a soft kiss on the top of her head and eased his arm out from under her, careful not to wake her. Then he moved silently from the bedroom, closing the door behind him so the call he'd make from the kitchen telephone didn't rob him of the pleasure of rousing her with more kisses and a little exploration of that body he was itching to get his hands on again.

The small living room was awash in sunshine when he got there. Since the drapes on the picture window hadn't been pulled and exposing himself to every passerby had no appeal, he retrieved his jeans and slipped them on.

Then he headed for the kitchen.

But he was barely a foot from the phone in there when he heard a knock on the front door.

He didn't have any idea who it could be, but he knew he didn't want anyone but him waking Tallie up, so he spun on his heels, retraced his steps and answered the knock.

"Mr. McDermot? Is that you?" the teenage boy on the other side of the door greeted Ry as if he couldn't believe his eyes. But then, in a small town, most folks knew everyone and where they ought to be early on a Monday morning.

And where Ry was supposed to be was not at Tallie Shanahan's house. In nothing but a pair of barely zipped blue jeans.

But Ry kept his cool in the face of the boy's astonishment. "Hey, Pete," he said, glancing at the huge array of brightly colored balloons the young man was carrying. "What can I do for you?"

"Got these here balloons for Ms. Shanahan."

"I'll take 'em," Ry said as if this were an everyday event, digging his wallet out of his back pocket so he could tip the boy.

"Uh...these are from my Uncle Justin," Pete said, hesitating both to take the five-dollar bill Ry was offering and to hand over the balloons.

Ry hadn't known there was any connection between the teenager and Tallie's old flame. It also hadn't even occurred to him that her old flame had sent the balloons. But knowing it now hit him like a bucket of ice water thrown in his face.

Still, he forced himself not to show it.

"I'll see she gets them," he assured the boy.

Pete hesitated some more, clearly unsure what to do. But in the end he took the five and gave Ry the balloons, which were tied together with a big white satin ribbon.

"Uh...thanks for the tip," Pete said then, not

sounding any more certain of himself now than he had before.

"Sure," was all Ry answered as he pulled the balloons inside and closed the door.

That's when he saw that what he was holding was not only balloons. Tied into the string of one of them—the only white one in the bunch— was a ring. A pear-shaped solitaire diamond on a thin white-gold band.

An engagement ring.

And connected to that—not in an envelope but out in plain sight—was a gift card.

All the arrangements are made. We can be married two weeks after you get here. There's a plane ticket waiting for you at the airport. I love you.

Justin

For a while Ry just stayed frozen to that spot, holding those balloons, reading and rereading the card, staring at the ring. It seemed as if time stood still. Or maybe it moved backward. Three years backward.

And all he could think was that he'd made the mistake of getting involved with someone who wasn't completely free. Again.

It didn't help that he reminded himself that he'd gone into this relationship with Tallie with his eyes open and should have been prepared for this possibility. It didn't help to remember that she'd been honest about her weakness for the other man rather than hiding it the way Shelly had hidden her connection to Dirk. None of that made it any easier now, when by design or not, it looked as if he'd been the pawn of sorts in yet another couple's games.

How could any one man be so damned stupid and gullible twice in a row? he asked himself.

And this time he'd even had warnings. The whole town had told him she'd likely go back to the guy she'd been with since she was a young girl. But had he taken heed?

Oh, no, not him. The best he'd done was to tell himself to keep his eyes open as he gave in to the attraction to her. Big deal. Because even with his eyes open he hadn't seen the truth. He hadn't paid attention to it.

Like just last night when he'd asked her if she was staying in Elk Creek for good. "I think so," she'd said. Not an unequivocal yes. But had he seen it for the hedging it now seemed to be? No. He'd just passed over it as if she'd given the right answer.

And had he persisted in finding out what had come of the phone call Saturday? Because if he had, maybe he would have learned that she hadn't told the other guy that they were finished once and for all—as she obviously hadn't or he wouldn't have sent the ring and the plane ticket. Maybe she hadn't even hedged with this Justin. Maybe she'd out and out accepted his proposal and if Ry had insisted on her talking about it she might have told him.

Had she accepted the other guy's proposal?

That note attached to the balloons certainly made it seem possible. If not likely.

But would she have agreed to marry somebody else and then spent the last two nights with Ry—Saturday night on his hall floor nearly making love and last night...

Lord, was it possible the Tallie he knew would do something like that?

It was hard to believe, even with all the painful things rushing through him at that moment.

But then he also reminded himself that Shelly had done it. Shelly had used him to sway the man she really wanted into doing what she hadn't been able to get him to do any other way. And then Shelly had had just one last fling with Ry before telling him in bed the next morning that she was marrying his best friend.

Maybe that's all the past twelve hours had been with Tallie, too. One last fling...

Ry suddenly knew he had to get the hell out of there. Before he got any angrier than he already was. Before he had to hear her tell him to his face that this had all been nothing more than a good time to her.

He let go of the balloons so they could float to the ceiling. Then, wishing he'd listened to his own alarms along the way, he yanked on his boots and searched through the discarded couch cushions for his shirt.

It took him a moment to recall that Tallie had worn it into the bedroom when they'd made the room change in the middle of the night.

And that was all the prompting required for another image to flood into his mind. The image of how incredibly appealing she'd looked in his shirt and what it had been like to slowly unfasten the buttons and ease it off her shoulders so it could float down around her feet and leave her standing naked before him...

He closed his eyes and went to war to get that picture out of his head. That was the last thing he needed to be thinking about.

But how was he going to go back into that bedroom where thoughts just like that, memories of everything that had happened there, waited to torture him?

Maybe he should just leave the damned shirt.

But it was bad enough that he was apt to be a laughingstock when word got around that he'd been there to accept her engagement ring from

another man. He didn't want to add to the talk
by being seen leaving her house half-dressed.

He shot another glance upward at those balloons, at that ring and the card that went with
it, and forced himself to think of Tallie mull-
ing over another man's proposal and still letting him make love to her, still letting him talk
about beginnings, agreeing that that was what
she wanted, too, when it might not have been
true.

His jaw clenched. The muscles in his shoulders were so bunched he could have lifted a
building on them. And he mentally slammed
shut that door to his heart, imagining Tallie
locked securely and forever on the outside of it.

Only then did he go back to the bedroom.

TALLIE WASN'T SURE what woke her, but she had
an almost instant recollection of Ry and the fact
that he should have been in bed with her.

Squinting against the morning light in the
room, she discovered him bent over, snatching
his shirt from the floor where they'd left it in
the middle of the night. Before he'd swept her
up into his arms and carried her to bed to make
love to her with an abandon she'd never experienced before. An abandon she'd like to experience again. Right then…

"Hi," she said with a stretch that kept her

naked body still covered by the sheet as she took in the sight of his tight, perfect derriere in those black jeans and wished it were bare instead.

He glanced at her briefly, and she had the impression that it was more out of surprise that she was awake than anything else. Then he went on with what he was doing.

He stood—keeping his back to her—and shrugged into his shirt. "Mornin'," he said succinctly, gruffly.

Something was wrong, Tallie realized then, belatedly tuning in to the tension that was also in the room with them.

"Is everything okay?" she asked.

"Fine," he answered curtly.

"Is everything all right with Andrew?"

"Far as I know."

And apparently he wanted to play twenty questions rather than offer her any information willingly.

"Are you going home?" she ventured, growing more alarmed by the minute.

"Thought I would."

Each answer was cool, abrupt, aloof. With a formality that harked back to the way he'd treated her before that day he'd walked in with Andrew for the first time. He wasn't actually being rude. Just removed. But it was a slap in the face to Tallie, who had expected much,

much more after the night they'd just spent together.

Keeping the sheet tightly across her breasts, she eased up into a sitting position against the quilted headboard of her bed, feeling very vulnerable. And confused. And maybe a little hurt.

Still, she didn't want to believe what was happening, so she tried again.

"If chocolate torte doesn't sound good for breakfast, we could have something else. Banana splits? Or cookies or ice cream?" she joked, forcing a lighter tone to her voice than she felt.

"No, thanks," he responded as if she'd been serious.

"Or we don't have to eat at all...." she said softly then, smoothing the sheet over her legs in hopes of luring him back to bed. And of luring back the Ry who had emerged since Andrew's arrival.

But Ry kept his back to her as he fastened his shirt, rolled the sleeves to his elbows and jammed the tails into his jeans with vicious jabs.

"Gotta get home," he snapped.

"You're sure nothing's wrong?" she repeated, hating the forlorn tone that crept into her voice.

"Looks like things are pretty right for you," he said with a cutting edge to his own voice.

"What do you mean?"

He finally turned toward her, but only enough to glance at her over his shoulder. A glance that came from beneath furrowed brows, from eyes that were as cold as any she'd ever seen. "Nothin'. Doesn't mean a thing in the world. Not much does when you come right down to it, does it?" he answered inexplicably, completely baffling her.

And then he just walked out. He didn't say goodbye. He didn't say *See you later.* Or *I'll call you.* He just walked out. Out of her bedroom, through the living room and out the front door, closing it resoundingly behind him. And leaving Tallie dumbfounded.

"So much for this being only the beginning for us," she murmured to herself.

Had those been merely empty words? she wondered. Had everything they'd shared the night before meant nothing? Had making love been just a roll in the hay to him?

Certainly it had meant more to her. A whole lot more. And she'd believed him when he'd said it was only the beginning for them. She'd counted on that. She'd believed and counted on everything he'd said.

She'd believed in him.

To such an extent that she remembered falling asleep after that first time of lovemaking feeling cared for, safe, secure. And full of expectations for more to come. More than a second round of lovemaking and then watching him walk out the door without so much as a thank-you-ma'am this morning.

Had she read too much into things? Had she taken what he'd said too literally? Too seriously?

She'd had a history of that with Justin. It was how their relationship had gone on for so long. Had she done it again with Ry?

It certainly seemed so. Because she had definitely thought last night was the start of something great between them. Something meaningful. Something long lasting.

But obviously he hadn't intended to have a future with her. He hadn't been as serious about them as she'd believed. The words, the declarations, must have come from the emotions of the moment. The desires that were on the verge of erupting. The passion.

But when those desires were satisfied, when the passion was spent? Apparently the words hadn't been anything but a lot of hot air.

And once again she'd let her expectations rise, only to have them shot down. To be disappointed.

Devastatingly disappointed. More disappointed than she'd ever felt with Justin.

That surprised her. After so many years of disappointments from Justin she thought she'd reached every level. Yet there she was, feeling even worse. And wondering why.

But when she really thought about it, she realized that a part of Justin had always been a fly-by-night—he made commitments to jobs, to living arrangements, that he didn't follow through on any more than he followed through with what he promised her. But nothing about Ry had seemed that way. And maybe because of that, without realizing she was doing it, she'd pinned stronger hopes on him. Because of that and maybe also because her feelings for Ry were different than anything she'd felt for Justin...

But whatever her feelings for Ry were, they seemed out of place in light of the way he'd just left. They seemed foolish. And bound to get her hurt.

Bound to?

She was already hurt.

But she didn't want to cry. She'd shed enough tears over broken promises from one man. She didn't want to be reduced to tears by yet another man.

She got out of bed with a vengeance and ripped the sheets from the mattress.

Fine. If that's how it was with Ry, that's how it was. She'd just go on. And be grateful that she hadn't wasted another fifteen years of her life on someone who didn't keep his word.

But resolves aside, by the time she'd thrown on her bathrobe and bundled up the bedding, tears were falling anyway.

Damn him! she thought as she carried the sheets out of the bedroom. Damn him! Damn him! Damn him!

But a few steps into the living room she caught sight of a huge spray of balloons hugging the ceiling.

Ry! was her first thought.

He must have been putting her on. Teasing her. Maybe, because it was already after eight, he'd needed to get home to Andrew, so maybe he'd gotten up early, bought her balloons and then only played a trick on her by acting like his old aloof self so she wouldn't anticipate his surprise.

She dropped the sheets on the spot and made a beeline for the balloons, feeling a full rush of joy and a whole new set of good things about him, even chastising herself for doubting him.

Until she pulled the balloons down and discovered the ring and the note.

From Justin.

Then she deflated all over again.

Because for some reason, the proposal, even yet another sign that Justin might really mean business this time, didn't touch her.

Instead it served to clarify something completely different.

That the balloons, the ring, the wedding plans, were from the wrong man.

And that the right man had left her high and dry.

TALLIE USED HER lunch break later that day to cross from the old Molner Mansion, which housed the medical facility, to the post office on the main floor of the courthouse just across the street. She'd ordered a new tabletop centrifuge for the office to spin blood samples and she'd received notice that it had arrived for pickup.

What she didn't take into account was the fact that by the time the humidifier-sized machine was wrapped in packaging to keep it safe and then boxed up, it made for a large, ungainly parcel for her to maneuver even a short distance.

She was struggling to push her way out the post office's separate entry with her rear end when, from outside, someone finally noticed her plight and pulled the door open for her.

The last person she expected that someone to be was Ry.

But once she managed to get herself and the boxed centrifuge out onto the sidewalk, that's just who she found holding the door for her— Ry, carrying Andrew on his hip and holding the handles of a plastic grocery sack with the same hand that braced the little boy.

"Oh," she said when her eyes met his. "Thanks," she added none too warmly, wishing she'd been left to her struggle rather than having to face him again so soon after their morning parting. Or maybe ever...

"Looks like you need some help," he said just as formally as he'd been at her house hours earlier.

"No, thanks. I'm fine," she answered, matching his aloofness and upping the ante with a heavy dose of the cold shoulder.

Two could play his game, she told herself. Besides, as she'd showered and dressed for work after he'd left, she'd decided not to open herself up for any more disappointments from him or any other man. She'd come to Elk Creek to escape just that and she wasn't going to step into yet another situation that seemed fraught with it. No matter how great-looking Ry was, standing there in work-worn jeans and a chambray shirt with the sleeves rolled up to muscle-bound biceps her hands itched to explore. No matter how sexy he was in those jeans that bulged slightly just to the left of the zipper with parts of him she now knew intimately...and yearned unwillingly to know even more of. No matter how much her heart ached just seeing him...

But when Andrew perked up and said a bright "Hi!" she could hardly snub him, too.

"Hi, sweetheart," she said in a far friendlier tone.

The baby's blond hair was clinging to his head, damp with sweat. And no wonder since the first heat wave of the summer had hit suddenly, raising the June day's temperature to ninety-five, and he was dressed in blue jeans of his own, miniature hiking boots and a tiny replica of a jean jacket over a red T-shirt Tallie could see peeking from beneath it. He was dressed for late October, not for June, and although she wanted to cut this encounter short—both to get away from Ry and her feelings for him, and to get the centrifuge to the office and out of her arms as soon as possible—she decided one more parenting lesson was in order.

She shifted the box in an attempt to redistribute some of the weight and said curtly to Ry, "It's too hot a day to have him in so many clothes."

"You're talkin' to the wrong guy about that. He dragged this stuff out of his drawer this mornin', and nobody could dare put anything else on him."

"Mine!" Andrew affirmed with a chubby hand pressed to his chest as if to ward off anyone thinking to remove the jean jacket.

"I've tried ten times to take the damned thing off but—"

"No wuy!" Andrew said before Ry could finish his sentence.

"It's a nice jacket, all right," Tallie said in the friendly tone again, speaking to Andrew. "And you can sure keep wearing it. You just won't be able to eat those grapes while you have it on," she said nonchalantly, nodding at the green grapes sticking out of Ry's grocery bag, the same green grapes Andrew was trying—and failing—to reach.

Andrew gave her a slight frown, looked down at the grapes again and then tried to wiggle out of the coat. "Okay. Awl done."

That made both Ry and Tallie laugh in spite of themselves.

Ry set the grocery sack on the sidewalk and then Andrew beside it so he could take off the jacket.

"Make sure you break the grapes in half for him so he doesn't choke on them," she said as he removed Andrew's jacket.

Then, thinking of the way Ry had walked out on her that morning, she headed for her own destination without so much as a goodbye.

"Hey!" he shouted to stop her as soon as he noticed she was on the move. "I'll give you a hand with that package."

"I'm fine," she called back, not turning to even glance at him.

"Tallie..." he called again for no reason she could fathom, and this time she pretended not to hear him as she crossed the street.

Two could definitely play his game.

"Uh...am I mistaken or did you just get the brush-off?"

Shane's voice came from behind Ry as he stood on the street corner, watching Tallie walk away.

"Appears so," Ry answered, never taking his eyes off her as she crossed the street, letting his glance follow her all the way to the front door of the Molner Mansion where Brett Johnson from the hardware store met up with her, apparently offered to carry the box for her and was obviously rewarded with the package, a smile that made Ry's insides melt and a thank-you that looked as sweet as sugar.

And as he stood there staring even after the two of them had disappeared into the medical building, he recognized what a blow it had been for him to be met with her bare civility and to see her clear desire to get away from him as quickly as she could.

Even if it hadn't been all that different from

the way he'd acted that morning, and even if he did have it coming, it still stung.

"She probably doesn't feel the need to bother bein' friendly now that she'll go off to Alaska to marry that old flame of hers and put all of Elk Creek behind her again," Ry reasoned in further response to his brother's comment.

"She seemed pretty friendly to Brett over there," Shane pointed out with a poke of his chin in the direction of the medical building's entrance.

Ry ignored that, finding a diversion in Andrew, who was sitting on the sidewalk trying to take off his hiking boots.

"You have to leave those on," he said more harshly than he'd intended to.

It didn't phase Andrew as he went on tugging at them. "Hot," he said, apparently opting for stripping down completely now that he'd been persuaded to remove even a portion of the clothes he'd demanded to wear.

Ry grabbed the grocery sack and picked up Andrew again before the tot could pull his shirt off—as he was trying to do once he realized he couldn't untie the double knots in his shoelaces.

"Not here, little man. You can undress in the truck if you're too hot," he said, forcing a milder tone into his voice and heading for the parking lot near the courthouse where he and Shane had parked.

Shane fell into step beside him, saying as he did, "I...uh...heard that Tallie got an engagement ring from that guy everybody around here talks about."

"This mornin'," Ry confirmed what he hadn't told anyone about before.

"While you were there?"

"I answered the doorbell when it rang and accepted the balloons that came with it."

"Nice of you."

"Mmm," Ry grumbled.

They'd reached his truck by then and once he'd deposited the groceries behind the seat, he set Andrew down and pulled off the hiking boots and the little boy's jeans, leaving him in only his diaper and T-shirt. He put him in the car seat the two men had roped securely into the center of the truck's bench seat to replace the seat belts that didn't exist there and then got in behind the wheel as his brother took up the passenger's side.

"That why you came home in such a foul mood today?" Shane asked.

"History repeats itself," Ry said under his breath.

"She slept with you last night and accepted some other guy's proposal this mornin'?"

"I imagine so."

"You *imagine* so? Don't you know?"

"I know she slept with me last night."

"But you don't know about the proposal?"

"Didn't stick around for that part."

"Why the hell not?"

"I've been through that scene once before. Didn't want a rerun of it. I put on my pants and took off."

"Then you don't know if she accepted or not."

"It's what she's wanted from the guy since she was a girl. Why wouldn't she accept it?"

"How 'bout because of you?"

"Yeah, we know how my luck runs in *that* arena. I'm the one they use to make the other guy jealous enough to pop the question, not the guy they end up with," Ry said as he drove too fast down the country road that led to their ranch.

"This is all about Shelly and Dirk, isn't it?"

"I'd say it's all about my bein' stupid twice."

"I think you made a mistake walkin' out before you knew where Tallie stood on this. Things may look the same, but she seems a whole lot different than Shelly was."

"You only met Shelly that one weekend when you came down to visit, there at the end."

"Yeah, and she rubbed me wrong. Made a pass at me—I never told you about it."

Ry cast a frown at his brother. "Why the hell didn't you tell me?"

"Man, I didn't know what to do. She had you so snowed I wasn't sure you'd believe me. Then, about the time I decided to take my chances and tell you, she told you she was marryin' Dirk. I knew it hurt you, but I always thought you dodged the bullet on that whole deal."

"And you didn't tell me even after the fact?"

"Seemed like rubbin' salt in the wound. But I'm tellin' you now because Tallie seems like a totally different kind of woman. One you shouldn't let go without a fight. Remember that Maya told you Tallie'd never so much as kissed another man till you. If she went all the way to sleepin' with you, I'd say there's more goin' on than the kind of thing that went on with Shelly."

"Shelly slept with me," Ry reminded wryly.

"I think Shelly would have slept with a barnyard dog—no offense. Tallie's not the same. And if you slept with her last night, then hightailed it out of her place this mornin' like it didn't mean much to you, it's no wonder she didn't want to give you the time of day over at the courthouse. Hell, you're liable to have pushed her right into that other guy's arms treatin' her like that the one and only time she let somebody else get close. I hate to tell you, but I'm thinkin' you didn't make a smart move this mornin'."

They'd reached the ranch by then, and Ry pulled to a stop in front of the house. His thoughts were racing a mile a minute—partly with all his brother had said to him and partly with images of Tallie smiling up at the hardware salesman outside of the medical building.

He knew Brett Johnson wasn't his competition, but since he'd never met the man who was, somehow Brett got to be the proxy for the other man in Ry's mind. It was as if he'd been watching her with Justin. And just imagining her with another man so vividly was even more of a blow than the delivery of the ring had been. More of a blow than her treatment of him on the street corner.

Tallie with another man...

It was like a knife stab to his gut.

Even if she had a long history with Justin, even if the whole town talked as if she and Justin belonged together, Ry couldn't stand the idea. He couldn't believe it was right for her.

How could it be when *he* was right for her...

So don't let her go without a fight, he told himself as he recalled his brother's words.

"You all right?" Shane asked as he opened the truck's passenger's door to get out.

"I think I need a minute," Ry answered.

"I'll take the boy inside," Shane offered, releasing Andrew from his car seat and carrying the baby into the house while Ry stayed where he was, sitting behind the steering wheel, staring straight ahead, lost in thought.

Should he put up a fight for Tallie?

He'd let Shelly go without one. He hadn't even considered putting up any kind of struggle for her since it was clear she'd only used him. Besides, his feelings for her had turned so cold when he'd found out what she'd done, he hadn't wanted her anymore.

Yet not only was Shane right that Tallie was nothing like Shelly, but his brother was also right about the disparity in the circumstances.

When he really thought about it, he didn't believe Tallie was just using him. She wasn't that kind of person. And she wasn't a liar, either, so when she'd told him her feelings for the other man had changed, that she wanted to break the pattern with him, to stay away from him, Ry knew she'd meant it.

Plus hadn't she said that she'd left the other guy because she'd come to the point where she wasn't sure she'd have accepted him even if he did finally want to make the commitment?

He'd forgotten about all that until that moment. And remembering it made him wonder if maybe she *hadn't* accepted the other guy's proposal after all. If maybe the other guy was assuming something he shouldn't have assumed in sending that ring and the note that had come with it.

"And maybe I've done some assuming I shouldn't have, too...." he murmured to himself.

Then he hit the steering wheel with both hands and enough anger to make the truck bounce, shouting, "Damn!"

No, Shelly hadn't been worth fighting for. But Tallie was most definitely a different story.

One other thing was different, too, he realized as he turned the key in the ignition and started the engine again.

He loved Tallie. He loved her more than he'd ever loved Shelly. Which was why even all the bad things he'd been thinking about since that morning hadn't turned off his feelings for her the way Shelly's actions had turned off his feelings for her.

Because even if Tallie had accepted the other man's proposal, Ry still wanted her.

He wanted her enough to fight for her.

If it wasn't too late...

Chapter Nine

After retrieving the centrifuge from the post office, Tallie had enough of her lunch break left to make a trip home.

Between waking up to find Ry a changed man that morning and meeting him on the street midday, her stomach was so tied in knots that she couldn't eat, but she fixed herself a glass of iced tea and took it with her into the living room.

She sat on the overstuffed chair rather than the couch. She wasn't sure she'd ever be able to use the couch again without reliving what had happened there the night before. And being tortured by desires that were once more uncalled-for.

The engagement ring Justin had sent was on the end table beside the chair and it caught her eye. She hadn't paid much attention to it when she'd come out of the bedroom after Ry had left. Thinking about him and his fast retreat, she'd barely done more than free the ring from the balloons and set it on the table for safekeeping.

But now she picked it up and studied it.

It was a beautiful ring. With a diamond large enough to have cost Justin six months' salary. A pear-shaped solitaire set in white gold—just what she'd always said she wanted.

Curiosity caused her to slip it on her finger. It was a little large and with the weight of the stone she had to hold it in place with her other hand as she stretched out her arm to see how it looked.

No doubt about it—the ring was gorgeous.

But the only thing it stirred in her was a sinking feeling.

A movement outside drew her attention to the entryway, and through her open front door she saw Ry climb the steps to her porch and walk up to the screen.

Through the wire mesh he looked from her to her outstretched hand with the ring still on it and back to her face before he said, "Hi."

She dropped her hands to her lap self-consciously even as she considered not answering his greeting and making a beeline across the entry to slam the wooden door closed in his face. She considered ranting and raving and telling him to go away, to leave her alone, never to speak to her again because she didn't want anything to do with him.

But there he was in those jeans and that chambray shirt and those bulging biceps and hard thighs and big hands and chiseled face and vibrant green eyes and sun-shot hair. And instead she got up from her chair and walked over to the door.

"Forget something this morning?" she said, still no more warmly than on the street corner shortly before. Sarcastically, in fact.

"A few things," he answered. "Can I come in?"

She just shrugged, wondering if tormenting her with these meetings was his idea or just fate toying with her. But one way or another, as he opened the screen and let himself in, she worked to shore up her defenses against him.

Tallie spun on her heels and returned to the living room, not inviting Ry to come along.

He followed her anyway, and when she faced him again she stood completely behind the chair she'd been sitting in earlier, purposely putting it between them.

"I didn't come across anything that was yours when I straightened up," she informed him bluntly.

"Belongings aren't what I forgot."

"What did you forget, then?" she asked with a challenging upward tilt of her chin.

"I forgot that you are who you are."

"Who did you think I was?"

"I forgot that you aren't Shelly," he said calmly, patiently, ignoring Tallie's continuing coolness. "I forgot what kind of person you are. And what you'd told me about yourself, about how things were with you and with that other guy—" He nodded down at her hands where they clasped the back of the chair, the engagement ring still on her finger. "I saw that ring and the note and I guess I had a sort of flashback. I lost sight of everything else. And figured you'd gotten what you'd wanted, from the man you wanted it from—like Shelly."

"And now you're here to offer congratulations?" Tallie said, still not nicely. He'd hurt her too much to easily wash it away.

"No, I'm not here to offer congratulations. Even if it's called for." He shifted his weight to one insolently sexy hip, jammed his hands through his hair and then slid them both into his pockets just to the knuckles, leaving his thumbs out and pointed at the zipper she didn't want to be distracted by.

Then he said, "When the end came with Shelly and I found out that our whole relationship had been a plan on her part just to make

Dirk jealous, I shut off and left them to each other. I didn't try to convince her otherwise or woo her or win her away from him because I didn't want her then. But this mornin', even thinking maybe you'd done the same thing, I didn't feel that way. I was reelin', don't get me wrong. And mad and—well, all that stuff you saw in the way I behaved. But it still didn't change my feelings for you. It didn't keep me from wantin' you. And that clued me in to just what my feelin's for you are." He pinned her with those kiwi-colored eyes. "I'm in love with you, Tallie. In a way I wasn't with Shelly."

"Oh." Tallie knew she sounded dim-witted, but he'd shocked her so completely she was at a loss for words.

Before she could regain her wits, he went on. "That made me start to thinkin' about a lot of things I'd forgotten, and it occurred to me that I could have jumped the gun here this mornin'. That maybe you hadn't accepted that guy's proposal and then just had one last fling with me for fun—"

"That's what you thought?"

"The flashback, remember? That's what Shelly did, and the minute I saw that ring and read the card that made it sound like you'd already agreed to marry the other guy, yeah, that's what I thought. But after thinkin' through some of this stuff, I started to wonder if maybe that other guy had just assumed that because of the way things have always been with the two of you, that those balloons and that ring and a gung-ho attitude were all it would take to get you back again. But that maybe he was wrong. That just maybe if I hadn't been a jerk today, if I'd put up the fight for you that I never bothered to put up for Shelly—"

Tallie's pager went off like a gong in the quiet somber of the room and stopped him short.

Of all the bad timing in the world, Tallie was convinced this had to be the worst.

But there her pager was, hooked onto the belt of her jeans, beeping to beat the band.

And when Tallie looked down at the pager's display as she turned it off, she saw the code that told her it was an emergency.

"I have to take this," she said, knowing that since she was the only medic in town delaying could mean the difference between life and death for someone.

"Great," Ry said, closing his eyes, scrunching up his forehead and sighing with what sounded like frustration.

But there was nothing she could do as the pager went off again, making it clear that whatever she was needed for she'd better hurry.

She rushed into the kitchen to use the phone

there to call the office, getting through on the second ring. Ry was still in the middle of her living room when she finished with the call moments later and returned.

"Sonny Rordin's been kicked in the chest by a horse. I have to get out to him right now," she informed Ry, no longer as contrary as she'd been.

"Sure," he agreed solemnly, reluctantly. "We can finish this later."

Tallie didn't know what else to say. Her thoughts were in a jumble, too many feelings were running rampant through her and she had no time to sort through any of it, any of what he'd said so far, any of her own responses. She just had to get out of there and to the young boy in need of her help.

But the one thing she did do before she went out the door Ry held open for her was remove Justin's ring from her finger and replace it on the end table.

At that moment it was as good a message as she could come up with.

And then it was Tallie who left Ry to just watch her go for the second time that day.

It was a long afternoon and evening for Tallie.

The eleven-year-old boy she'd rushed out of her house to aid was seriously injured when she'd reached him in the field where the acci-

dent had happened. As near as she'd been able
to tell, he'd suffered broken ribs that had punc-
tured his lung and other internal injuries she'd
only guessed at.

He'd needed more care than she could provide, so she'd called the hospital in Cheyenne
that ordinarily sent a helicopter in dire emer-
gencies when time was of the essence and even
a speeding ambulance couldn't get a patient to
more complete care fast enough.

But when she'd called for the helicopter, she
was told a multiple-car wreck outside of the city
had all transports occupied.

Thinking quickly, she'd enlisted Jackson
Heller's help and helicopter to perform the service. But without the emergency medical techni-
cians that came onboard the hospital helicopter,
she needed to fly into Cheyenne with the Ror-
dins to keep Sonny alive along the way.

Between the trip there, the time she'd spent
making sure her patient was cared for in the already overwhelmed E.R. and staying with the
family until the boy was stabilized in the in-
tensive-care unit, it was late that night before
Jackson flew her home. Late that night before
she had a minute to herself to think about Ry
and his declaration that afternoon.

But in the droning of the helicopter's engine

and the dark of the night sky, there was nothing else she could think about.

Uppermost in her mind was how she felt about all that Ry had said. About him.

There was no denying his actions had scared her off that morning. Having been singed by the flame of unkept promises and unmet expectations in the past, Ry's sudden change, his walking out on her after the night they'd spent together, after what had seemed like a vow that it was only the beginning for them, had felt like the heat from the same flame. And that made her leery of him. Of everything he'd said.

She knew too well how easy it was to fall under the spell of a sweet-talking man. To be convinced by what he said in heartfelt words. To believe him.

And then to find out that those heartfelt words were as far as it was likely to go.

Even now, with Justin's ring sitting on her end table at home, she knew there was a fair chance that if she was to accept it and fly back to Alaska, no wedding would actually take place.

But what about Ry? Were one morning's actions an isolated occurrence or were they a sign that he was just like Justin?

She thought long and hard about that. But she finally came to the conclusion that Ry and

Justin weren't alike. Not in any way she could come up with.

Ry wasn't the kind of person who would string her along for his own sake the way Justin had. He wasn't a man who ran from responsibility or commitment—he even kept promises he *didn't* make, like taking on Andrew's guardianship.

She recalled his telling her that he was a putting-down-roots kind of guy. Which made him a good choice for Andrew's guardian, but didn't it also make him a man who stuck with more than a place? Who stuck to his word, too?

She thought it did.

He was also the kind of man who had taken a leave of absence from his own life to work the ranch of a friend in need. The kind of man who had disconnected from the deep-seated pain caused by other people to take on the raising of their orphaned son when he could have as easily—and understandably—refused the burden pressed upon him. And having accepted that burden, he'd bent over backward to do right by the boy.

And as for the return of his earlier aloofness and formality? She knew now that was how he protected himself. It wasn't the real Ry. It wasn't an indication of a man like Justin who held just enough of himself in escrow to never really commit to a relationship.

No, the closer the helicopter got to Elk Creek, the more Tallie knew that the good things she'd learned about Ry since meeting him, the good things she'd thought—and felt—about him, were the right and true things regardless of what had happened that morning. His leaving had had everything to do with the delivery of Justin's ring and the flashback it had sent him into, and nothing to do with the man himself.

When it came right down to it, she believed that Ry McDermot was someone she could trust. Someone she could give herself to. Someone she could love freely and openly and without reservation.

Which was a good thing because she knew with sudden clarity that Ry McDermot was the man she loved. With all her heart. More deeply than she'd loved Justin. Because, she realized at that moment, there had been a part of herself she'd held in escrow from Justin, too. To shield herself in some small way after so many lessons in how unreliable he was.

But even as she'd tried to hold herself apart from Ry, she hadn't been able to. She'd still fallen in love with him.

And suddenly what she wanted more than air to breathe was to get to him. To hear him finish what he'd begun in her living room that afternoon. To tell him she loved him, too.

She turned to Jackson, whom she'd known since they were children growing up together in Elk Creek, and who had left her to her own musings since the return trip began. "How long till we get back?" she asked.

"About twenty more minutes," he answered after checking his control panel and peering out the windows as if he could tell where they were just by looking at the open countryside over which they were flying.

Twenty minutes. It didn't sound like a long time. But it felt like an eternity.

"Any chance that we could make an undesignated stop?"

A HELICOPTER DID not make for a quiet entrance. Especially not with the beaming headlight that illuminated the ground below so a safe landing could be achieved.

By the time the aircraft had touched down on the driveway in front of the McDermot ranch, the whole household—minus Andrew—was watching.

Shane had his arm around Maya—both of them in bathrobes—standing on the front end of the veranda on the side of the house where their bedroom was. Buzz was braced by his walker in the open front door, wearing boxer shorts, his cowboy boots and his hat—but no teeth. And Ry stood on the lawn dressed in a pair of jeans, without a shirt or shoes.

"Thanks, Jackson!" Tallie called over the noise before she got out of the copter and quickly cleared the rotor blades so he could take off again.

"Anythin' wrong?" Buzz hollered to Tallie over the uproar as she headed for Ry.

"I hope not," she called back without taking her eyes off her goal.

Ry just stayed put, watching her come, his hands on his hips where the jeans rode low, his bare feet spread apart.

"So. You were saying…" she shouted over the din of the rising helicopter, greeting him as if only a moment's interruption had stalled what he'd been telling her that afternoon.

It made him smile. And to Tallie that smile was better than any diamond ring.

He took hold of her elbow then. "Come with me," he said, guiding her to the porch on the opposite side of the house from the wing that encompassed Shane's and Maya's rooms. He led her all the way to the outside door of his suite, right into his bedroom.

His bed was still made. Tallie shied away from looking at it and faced Ry—who was closer behind her than she'd thought—focusing on his handsome features and the fact that he was freshly shaved, as if he'd expected her.

Without thinking about it, she reached out and ran the fingertips of one hand along his smooth jawline. "Were you going somewhere?"

"Your place. I gave up callin' about half an hour ago, thought I'd go see if you were there and just not answerin' your phone."

"I've been in Cheyenne since I left home this afternoon," she said, going on to explain all that had happened with Sonny Rordin and that, although he was severely hurt, he'd be all right.

Then she glanced at the door that connected Ry's bedroom with Andrew's and said, "Since I don't hear a peep out of him, I guess Andrew's asleep?"

"I don't know how, with all that racket, but he seems to be."

That was enough chitchat, Tallie decided, eager to get down to brass tacks. "So let's pretend I've just come home and found you on my porch. What would you be saying to me right now?"

"Better yet, what'd you fly in here to say to me?" he countered.

Ah, he wasn't going to be the only one to take the risk. He'd gone out on a limb that afternoon, and now it was her turn.

He took her hand from where it had fallen to her side after caressing his cheek—even though she'd rather it had fallen to the mounds of pectorals taunting her with their bare, masculine beauty.

"Still no ring, I see," he said to urge her on.

"That's because I'm not accepting it. Or Justin. Or his proposal. I could have told you that this morning if you'd have let me."

"And puttin' it on this afternoon? What was that about, then?"

"It was just like trying it on in a jewelry store. Curiosity."

"You weren't even tempted?"

"After last night? What I was, was disappointed. I counted on that promise you made that this was only the beginning for us, and then you played Jekyll and Hyde, and caused me a few flashbacks of my own."

"I'm sorry."

"You should be."

"But here you are," he prompted, apparently determined to know what she was thinking, feeling.

"Here I am because I love you, you big dope," she finally admitted. "Because I meant it when I told you I wanted last night to be the beginning, too. Because the minute I saw that ring and realized it was from Justin, I knew it was the right sentiment from the wrong man."

A small satisfied smile teased Ry's lips as he pulled her into his arms.

Tallie had more to say. And much more she wanted to hear from him. But when his mouth captured hers, she lost track of it all and melted into the strong arms that came around her. She wrapped her arms around him so she could lay her palms to the wide expanse of his back, to press her breasts to that magnificent chest of his.

Passion was only a quarter step away, the bed a little farther, but as Ry unfastened buttons and snaps and zippers and rid them both of their clothes, he eased her in that direction, too.

Not that she was unwilling. Every nerve in her body, every sense was tuned in to him, to the silken feel of his taut flesh over hard muscle, to the warm sweetness of his mouth over hers, his tongue boldly toying and teasing and tormenting, to the clean scent of after-shave that made her giddy, to the soft sounds of pleasure escaping from his throat—and hers.

They let their bodies say the rest as each explored the other, learning, arousing, pleasing all over again. They moved together in perfect harmony, perfect unison, perfect bliss, as desire pushed them to a frenzied pace, as hunger drew them together with an urgency that belied the fact that they'd indulged in hours of lovemaking only a short time before.

Breaths mingled. Bodies meshed and joined. And hearts seemed to soar as they once more climbed to a peak of ecstasy so exquisite, so flawless, so earth-shatteringly wonderful that nothing but a love shared deeply and genuinely could have brought them to it.

Exhausted, satiated and still tangled together, Ry rolled to his back and pulled Tallie to lie on top of him with her head resting on his chest and every curve and hollow of her body finding the answering hollow and curve of his.

"I love you, Tallie," he said then, putting the finishing touches to what she'd wanted to hear from him all along.

"I love you, too."

"We're lucky that our damned pasts didn't ruin it."

"Mmm. Just promise me—"

"Anything. Everything. I promise to love and cherish you forever and a day. To give you the sun and the moon and the stars. To be with you as long as I live," he said as if repeating wedding vows.

"And?" she said.

He laughed, vibrating beneath her. "You want more?" he joked, sounding astonished.

"I want you to marry me."

"I thought that went without saying."

"Not quite."

"Then I'll say it—will you marry me?"

"When?"

"As soon as possible. Tomorrow or the next day or the next or whenever it can be arranged around blood tests and licenses." He gave her a gentle swat on the rump. "But not before you send that ring back."

"First thing in the morning."

He kissed the top of her head and arched his hips up into hers with a message she was only too happy to receive. "Maybe not *first* thing," he said, his tone thick with insinuation.

Then in a husky, serious voice he said, "I really do love you."

"I really do love you," she answered with the same level of solemnity.

"Do you think Elk Creek can adjust to your being with me instead of old what's-his-name?"

"They'll have to, won't they?"

"Yes, ma'am, they will. How about you? Are you sure, after all this time with him—?"

She stopped Ry's words by rising up to kiss him as sensually as she knew how.

"I'm sure," she said when she thought she had him suitably breathless. "I've never been more sure of anything."

"You know you're takin' on a whole package—all the McDermots, Buzz, Andrew. We're a mixed bag."

"Good. I'll never get bored."

"And you're willing to be mama to Andrew?"

"Absolutely," she answered without having to consider it because she'd come to love the boy as much as the man. "But if there are other kids you're likely to inherit I'd like to be warned," she joked.

"I don't think there are any more I'm likely to inherit. But I was thinkin' about makin' a few of our own. Now that I'm so good at daddyin'."

Tallie flexed her hips down into his. "There are some things you're good at, but I'm not sure *daddyin'* is one of them just yet."

"Is that so? Maybe I should show you what I *am* good at, huh?"

"Again?" She pretended surprise even though his body had alerted her ahead of time.

"And again and again and again…"

He did just that then, making love to her once more with an renewed hunger and a playfulness that she hoped followed them throughout a lifetime together. A playfulness that carried over even after they'd worn each other out for good and settled in to sleep—he on his back, she up close to his side, using his shoulder as a pillow.

"You know," Ry warned, "I'm gonna be

tellin' folks until the day we die that you're the one who did the proposin' to me."

"And flew in by helicopter in the middle of the night to do it—don't forget that part."

"I don't think there's anything about you that I'll ever be forgettin'."

"I'm going to hold you to that."

"And to everything else, too. And welcome to it," he said with assurance. "I'll never let you down, Tallie."

"I know you won't," she whispered, kissing his chest. She heard him sigh as he dropped off to sleep, but before she drifted along behind him she couldn't help thinking something she would never have believed possible—that she was grateful for all of Justin's empty promises.

Because all those unkept promises, all those unmet expectations, all those disappointments, had kept her free to find in Ry a man who would never leave her hanging. A man who would fulfill her every need, her every desire.

A man who would give her the life she wanted, the family she wanted, the stability she wanted.

And more love than she'd ever hoped for or dreamed of.

* * * * *